COME
BACK

COME BACK

BACK

SKY GILBERT

A MISFIT BOOK

Published by ECW Press
2120 Queen Street East, Suite 200, Toronto, Ontario, Canada M4E 1E2
416.694.3348 | info@ecwpress.com

LIBRARY AND ARCHIVES CANADA CATALOGUING IN PUBLICATION

Gilbert, Sky
Come back / Sky Gilbert.

ISBN 978-1-77041-049-7
ALSO ISSUED AS: 978-1-77090-188-9 (PDF); 978-1-77090-189-6 (EPUB)

I. Title.

PS8563.I4743C66 2012   C813'.54   C2011-906972-5

Editor: Michael Holmes / a misFit book
Cover design: Rebecca Lown
Cover images: Ruby Red Slippers © mikeledray/shutterstock;
landscape before storm © Orientaly/shutterstock
Type: Troy Cunningham
Printing: Webcom   1   2   3   4   5

This is a work of fiction. Names, characters, places, and incidents either are the
product of the author's imagination or are used fictitiously, and any resemblance
to actual persons, living or dead, business establishments, events, or locales is
entirely coincidental.

The publication of *Come Back* has been generously supported by the Canada
Council for the Arts which last year invested $20.1 million in writing and publishing
throughout Canada, and by the Ontario Arts Council, an agency of the Government
of Ontario. We also acknowledge the financial support of the Government of Canada
through the Canada Book Fund for our publishing activities, and the contribution of
the Government of Ontario through the Ontario Book Publishing Tax Credit. The
marketing of this book was made possible with the support of the Ontario Media
Development Corporation.

PRINTED AND BOUND IN CANADA

MIX
Paper from
responsible sources
FSC® C004071
www.fsc.org

ANCIENT FOREST ™
FRIENDLY

for Ian

"My desire has invented new desires,
my body knows unheard-of songs."

—— Hélène Cixous,
The Laugh of the Medusa

Yes, I am aware that I should, perhaps, *not* go there. Even as I write, the word *sentiment* — or rather *sentimentality* — comes up like yesterday's dinner. Please believe me that there is no urge on my part to go back. It is long gone and I don't give a flying fuck. So I am slipping into my previous nomenclature. But I don't — I really don't — give a damn about any of it. Do you think I want to go back? When I think for a moment, it all returns. Like a flood, yes, but one I can control.

I see you, in my mind's eye, sitting there, smiling, looking satiric. When? When was it that I suggested something you considered very outrageous, and you said, "It seems that you have temporarily lost your mind"? And then you went on in that vein. You know, my darling, I wish you were not so ruled by your loins.

Is it that? You claim it is.

Of course, Johnny. But sometimes I think it is your heart, because that is the way we think of women — and you are one. But still. Let's just say it has nothing to do with being a woman. We both know that men too are puddles, and can dissolve even without menstruating.

Remember when you stopped menstruating? I do. You dove into bodybuilding with your usual innocent bravado — no reservations whatsoever. Then it was, "I want a period. I don't want to stop fucking menstruating. Jesus." Someday you will. Soon, actually. That is certainly a something I no longer regret. Perhaps it has to do with what I am going to tell you about. Because, Johnny, I am going to use you unabashedly as a sounding board. That's what you are best at when it comes to me, but I wouldn't be alive if it wasn't for you, so I suppose you are more than that to me. You know what I mean. You are what, barely fifty? And I am . . . so old, so very, very old. One cannot even imagine how old I am. And to have died so many times! When one has lived and died so often it does not seem quite so fantastical to get a little teary-eyed. It won't last. But yes, even after all these years there is a whiff. A friend of mine wrote a beautiful essay once called "A Whiff of Abandon." There's a whiff of abandon in me. It's still there, even though I cannot, or will not, act upon it. No, I have no real actual desire to climb onto one of those things, to straddle it again, or better yet to have it in my mouth. There is still the memory — but memory does not express it — the mood (it is in a way a mood) that overtakes one. But that sounds too romantic. There is a sense memory — the way actors talk about the remembrance of a smell, or a taste. Jesus, it's enough maybe to say there is still a longing for it — an appreciation of beauty that never goes away. One looks at the fall of a hand, or the turn of a head, or the veins in an arm, and one aches for it. And then I look at my own body: a too familiar tapestry of wires and scars and wrinkles. As I write this, my pacemaker dutifully ticks away the seconds. But they are not being counted — and that is a good thing too. So yes, I have the longings, always will, in this ridiculous non-body of mine. But that doesn't mean that — even if I immerse myself in all of the abandon — I will go back there.

So here it is: I want to talk about a new project of mine and, of course, I want your comments. But do remember it's only recently that I've been able to receive criticism without completely falling apart. You know where the falling apart comes from. We won't go there. So don't forget there's always *sensitivity*. I know you are ruthless, and that is what is so important about you. Of course, I value that. Remember that I am not just one of your students. (I am, but I'm not.)

The man I'm going to tell you about is, or was (sorry, he seems so alive on the page), estimable. By that I mean his talents can be very accurately estimated. He is typical of his time and era. That really is the reason one wants to write about anyone. He was, to some degree, the Samuel Pepys of his age, though he was not consciously chronicling anything but his own demise. On reading his work I am amazed at the pretentiousness of us all; of scholarship, certainly, but also of any other attempt to make sense of the world, give it pattern, structure. This is what they still like to call art. We know better, of course. (I sometimes wonder how long it will take the world to catch up.) He lived and died at a time when things still existed and mattered, and it was important to make choices. Of course, my musings have value only in the way that any historical reconstruction does; they will say more about me than him or anything else, for that matter, and are really being expressed only for my own amusement. So please, don't tell me they are useless.

Though you are so much younger than I am, you have abnegated your responsibility, refused to participate in the world. This makes sense for some, I suppose. But not, somehow, for me. I still must go out there and I am still amused at how they react, how they stare. Of course, the old don't ever go out. I still enjoy it, though — the way I once enjoyed a sequined dress. And people look at me with disapproval, annoyance, discomfort — I am not what they expected, not acting the way they would act. It's all quite pleasing. So at the very most, I hope you can take the time to respond and even disapprove. After all, there is something in your disapproval I enjoy. You get very stern and I wonder if you are as stern with the women you love — with the women who (pardon me) you toy with, but you never love.

But just indulge me, please. I have to go on a little about the Munchkins. I know you will think it a bad sign that I want to talk about them. Let's try not to think of things in terms of "bad signs." It's not useful. Also, it's something of a self-fulfilling prophecy. In other words, if you continue to think of me as a sort of case, then how will I not continue to be one? It's true that all your worry reassures me that you still you love me (because I know you worry about me; when you are stern it means you are worried). And as much as I appreciate being loved, I still must insist that being so careful with me — will I fall back again (as if I could)? — is a way of courting disaster, almost an expression of wanting it to happen (not that you do). So if I say that for a moment I would like to talk about them (the Munchkins), I hope you won't be alarmed, and I won't get an incriminating ful-mination about the dangers of even mentioning them. I mean, they still come up! They do.

I received an alert about them. I stand duly chastised — I know I should not want to be alerted to references to that old . . . world. A friend got me the alert function as a present and a contribution to my new "integration." (I'm sure you know more about it than I do; it's like the

Google alert of old, only it goes in the chip.) He is, I'm sure you would think, a dangerous friend. Yes, he knows about me — I don't know how he figured it out, actually. I thought all traces were gone. Perhaps the clue was that I was smoking a cigarette. It was only one. I had only one — and again, it won't do any good to rail against it. After all, I know the horrible things you do, or you have given me an inkling. The worst that can come of a cigarette, I think, is that the fact that I smoke it in a certain way — at least, according to this young man — might be noticed. He is extraordinarily sycophantic; I am, to him, an idol or even a god. Don't worry, he won't tell anyone. I have sworn him to secrecy, and he does everything I say. It's a pity I'm not attracted to him — although I am. But it just seems too dangerous to nurture the sad old sense memory of — what shall we call it — sensuality? Yes, that's palatable. He is mentally unbalanced. He has admitted it, in fact. Anyway, he is responsible — his name is Allworth — for the newly installed alert function. I'm sure I should disable it — who knows what stalker could discover my location.

So be it. The alert function came up with that hoary old tale about the hanging Munchkin — the one who can be seen in one frame, apparently dangling in shadow by the yellow brick road. Well, all I have to say is, Fuck them! There was no hanging fucking Munchkin! But there sure were one or two who were well-hung.

Jesus Christ, why do people always have to turn it into a tragedy? What are we going to do now? Have a memorial service for an imaginary hanging midget and wear fucking black armbands? Jesus Christ: *so they were short, so what?* That means we have to feel sorry for them? They didn't fucking feel sorry for them*selves*. No, let me tell you, it was a *party* for them *all the time*, and I am sick and fucking tired of being demonized for saying so. Nobody understands that it was a tribute to the goddamn Munchkins for me to say that. I was the first to treat them as people — not just a bunch of dolls! And it's not my fucking fault if no one can handle it when I tell it like it is!

The Lollipop Guild guy — I can't remember his name — was such a fucking pervert! I mean that in the nicest sense; I mean it as a compliment. You think women don't go for guys like that? I guess that's all part and parcel of the "women don't really like big cocks" bullshit. Size doesn't matter? Sure it doesn't matter, in a technical sense. But there's such a thing as a *fantasy*. Don't underestimate the power of fantasy that a really big cock can create. I mean, just looking at one could scare you. (But that's the way I used to want to be scared.) Anyway, this little fucking Munchkin had a dick of death, even for a normal-sized male. And he really liked scaring women with it. And need I tell you how much power there is in being a little guy who can just vanquish — I mean, really vanquish — a regular-sized woman with his goddamn member?

I know all this because he showed it to me. He was bragging about it and I said, "Honey, show it to me — you know everyone wants to see it." So we went behind one of the candy-cane trees, and he hauled it out, and I burst out laughing. I mean, you've got to laugh at a thing like that, because there's nothing else to do. The Lord giveth, and he taketh away. . . .

I laughed harder than the time Marlene played the records of her European tour for us. I told Carson this, I think. She played song after song for us — but they weren't "songs." You couldn't hear anything but applause! Now and then Marlene would go, "That's Frankfurt," or "That's Berlin." I was on the floor.

Anyway, back to the Munchkin. He ended up marrying this normal-sized woman, and I would have given anything to have been in a locker room with some guys when he stripped down. So yeah, yeah, I know — please don't tell me all of this does not bode well.

There's something I've been meaning to ask you, Johnny. Since when did you become my conscience? Is that all there is to being a lover? Because I know, deep down — even though we've never done it — that somewhere, somehow, we are lesbians. In the old-fashioned sense of the word. I mean, of course you have sex with women — but I am a lesbian *inside*. I know I am. And even though our friendship is only, these days — how did they used to say it? — deeply epistolary, there is that element. We both know it. And if, in fact, I am now a lesbian, even though I no longer have anything much resembling a body, it would seem that we are lovers and that when we speak (even though you are not here) you have become my conscience. So can we cut that out? I know you won't, so we might as well just keep the whole conscience thing going, because that's what two people do when they are in love. Let's just come to terms with that, as they used to say in self-help books; let's be *real* about that, as we used to say in the sixties. Yes, yes, you are going to chastise me and that's because you love me, and because I love you too — we're lesbians in that way.

Which brings me back to the man I was telling you about — the Samuel Pepys of his age, or . . . not. Okay, fine, do it: tell me I shouldn't even be thinking about, or writing about, this poor lonely guy, exploring his fucked-up psyche. Just tell me that. But if you have the right to scold, then I have the right to hear what you say but not listen. Of course I will listen, but I won't take it to heart. I still do have a heart. Which reminds me of . . . But *there* we will not go. Because I know, in your heart, because you definitely have one, somewhere, even though you deny it . . . I know in your heart you know I appreciate that you care about me even if I don't pay attention. Because I can't pay attention. And I will use my interest in this man, in his historic moment, as an excuse not to listen to your chiding — which I can already predict.

This is the first trace of him I've discovered. I found it in the archives at the University of Toronto. He was writing during the early part of the millennium when he lost his mind. Didn't we all, slowly but surely? It's pre-9/11. One of my friends — and he's a gay friend — he still archaically calls himself that (no, not the one who put me onto the alert function) — noticed that I call it "nine-one-one." But it's nine-eleven, isn't it? Well, I just think of it as one big emergency. . . . And we mark everything from that — the decline. Or should we *not* be Eurocentric, and call it "the ascendance"?

So how did I find out about this artist from the past that I wish to put before you? Well, I was searching these old theses for gay subject matter, and a very nice librarian named Kim found it for me.

There are nice librarians, as well as those who are not, as you well know. I sometimes prefer the bitter ones, because they don't talk your ear off and they're not enthusiasts. Kim is an in-between, but not tragically so: she is neither a bitter librarian nor an enthusiast, she is just someone who seems to enjoy her job — but not too much. She said, in an offhand way, "Oh, there's this Dash King stuff." I reacted immediately to the name. Dash King — now, there's a name for you. I remarked that it seemed like a theatrical moniker. She said, "Now, that is the odd thing — his name was the bane of his existence." In other words, because he was called Dash King and was involved in matters theatrical, people assumed his name was concocted for theatrical purposes. And we all know the effects of that (I won't go there) — the enormous fakery that begins (you can't remember when) and catapults you into a spasmodic nothingness and near death — at least, in my case.

"And," said Kim, with a cock of her head and very stylish glasses, "though Dash King sounds like a theatrical, made-up name, in fact it was not made up at all. It was his actual name — Dashiell King. It was typical of him," she continued, "to have a reputation for something he couldn't quite live up to."

"In other words, being a gothic liar?" I wondered, not knowing how the word *gothic* got in there.

Kim, good soul that she is, didn't seem to notice. "Dash King was not a name simply invented to inspire controversy, or to be put up in lights, but in reality his name." Then she went on about the fact that Dash had never actually produced a thesis because of his nervous breakdown and eventual death.

But there was this pile of papers. What a romance for those who still have the scholar in them! A pile of papers! "It's a thesis, or the beginning of a thesis and also the ending of one, because he couldn't go on," Kim said. It seemed odd to me that the university would have kept it, so I asked why. She said because of his historical value — as he was at one time a well-known director/writer/gay activist (at this my interest was piqued). And so it was archived more as the record of the demise of a minor person of minor import. Well, again, nothing excites scholars as much as the idea of papers of a minor import — papers that have been all but dismissed and read by no one.

So I have them; they are temporarily in my possession. I will dole them out deliberately, as best I can, to let you savour them. I know you will devour his sad story, if only because of your delicious misanthropy. We can look back on him now and we can have a good chuckle and think about how these things once meant something when now they mean nothing.

Which reminds me of The Golden Age of Hollywood . . . Need I say more? Shimmering images on celluloid . . . The end of the world is near enough that one wonders what the optimists have in mind. Most of MGM's historic output can be reduced to the size of a microchip, so it should be someone's duty, calling, to bury it somewhere — to save it. Perhaps that's *my* calling. The idea that I am a *classic* — can I tell you what that means? It means I am dead, petrified; I'm mummified. My remains are good only for prayer. Don't get me started about those who pray to me — but when you are prayed to, then you know your life has stultified, and the responses you are eliciting are coming from people who can no longer respond, people who go through the empty motion of clapping. Don't you think I know what the sound of a roomful of applause means? Nothing. Nada. Less than nada — a voluptuous panic of anticipation for a love that does not exist *in reality*. But now you will object that I am trying to convince myself that such thoughts no longer upset me. Oh well, yes, so be it. Who else is there to convince?

Here it is. The earliest papers I read were his last concerted attempt, it seems, at a traditional academic essay. It is not, as essays go, particularly good. There is only a touch of originality, too much of it we already know, too much from one source — but the T. S. Eliot analysis, for instance, is okay. Of course, it's all surrounded by the construction of "gayness," though that goes unstated. What's interesting is that the essay is written not to be about homosexuality at all — yet it is.

It was written at the end of queer studies at the beginning of the millennium. The academic jobs had all but disappeared, which suggests that the whole effort was futile from the outset. Again, there is something heroic about this — about the end of postmodernism. There is still the word *modern* in it, which is related to romanticism. It's about a nostalgia for a kind of passionate order/disorder, couched in a Foucauldian tone of distance. They wanted distance at the turn of the century, longed for it, but the irony is that they shouldn't have — again — romanticized it so much. For now we have it; it is here. And where are we?

In what follows, Dash ostensibly compares the Hamlets of Olivier and, oddly, Mel Gibson. The stated purpose is to clarify, or at least accentuate, the differences between them in terms of the effeminacy of Hamlet, and towards the end of the essay, Dash offers an analysis of the two performances — Olivier, of course, being the effeminate Hamlet and Gibson being the masculine. Here is Dash's conclusion:

> The difference between these interpretations of the closet scene exemplifies the fundamental difference between the movies and their approaches to the play's theme. Olivier's Hamlet kisses his mother passionately, obeying an impulse that he himself does not understand. By the end of the scene he has his head in her lap and is clearly relishing the attention from her — almost as if he has happily finally wrenched her away from Claudius and gotten her all to himself. Gibson's Hamlet is kissed by Glenn Close passionately, and he is clearly horrified, and attempts to move away from her. Olivier's Hamlet is not so much a stranger in a hostile world but trapped in a universe of his own creation, a world that horrifies him, and from which he can't escape. He is truly mad; the torturous universe that he lives in is the product of

his own intense and overwrought thinking. He is not only a man who cannot make up his mind, but a man who lives in his mind — and not necessarily on this earth.

As Hamlet says (in a phrase, which, though justly famous, is only to be found in the Folio) "nothing is good or bad but that thinking makes it so."[37] Gibson, on the other hand, takes Marcellus's "Something is rotten in the state of Denmark"[38] quite literally — his Hamlet is no modern anti-hero who has created a nightmare life from his own fevered imagination. Instead he is a noble, reasonable man struggling in an evil, disordered world. Gibson's Hamlet is certainly thoughtful, as well as a man of action. The difference is that his obviously uncompromising analytical brain is weighing evidence throughout the play, trying to figure out if, in fact, The Ghost has been telling him the truth. He clearly would act if he had enough evidence. He is a reasonable man (much like modern-day reasonable men) who will not believe a ghost (no matter how real that ghost seems) until he is sure the ghost's claims are actually true. These moments of evidence gathering and thought are quite clear in Act III, as Hamlet watches Claudius watching the play, and decides not to kill Claudius when he is praying.

Olivier, on the other hand, is a melancholic in the original Renaissance sense — a man who thinks too much about things in general. Olivier leads us along through Hamlet's thoughts and decisions to the point where he releases himself to fate, and brings us the achingly beautiful attack on Claudius. For Olivier's Hamlet flings himself

across the room from the stairs, and flies, literally
— like a bird or an avenging angel — finally giving
himself up to his inexorable fate. In other words,
even Olivier's final "act" is not so much an act as
a relinquishing of his will to live. It is a fall from
a great height (literally) and a graceful, eloquent,
melancholic release. In contrast, Mel Gibson, in
typical heroic fashion, clearly relishes his battle
with Laertes and his opportunity to kill Claudius.
His final calm is that of a man who has "done the
right thing" and, indeed, acted decisively — as a
masculine man always should.

Both the argument and the examples are sensible
enough, and to some degree obvious. But the essay dis-
guises two agendas: 1) a general nostalgia for queer politics, and 2) an obsession concerning the sexuality of
Shakespeare. Such notions, today, make us laugh; we no
longer speak of sexualities in this manner. When I called
you a lesbian earlier, we both knew what I was referring to.
Even though your object choice often swings to women,
that is not significant. Of course, I was being humorous,
or trying to be, about the idea that you carry yourself in
the way of, and with the redolence and aristocratic sense
memory, the whiff perhaps, of what used to be known as
a bull-dyke — the "masculine" woman who "favours" S/M
sexual practices. And you wear ties. It is very important
that you wear ties. Of course, it is very important to *me* that
you wear ties. I am, as always, a "bossy bottom," the very
worst kind; I am the girl getting fucked who won't shut up.
Oh, to imagine myself in this ghostly way — to conjure the
past — makes me laugh.

I am puffing on a cigarette now, and it seems impossible
that anyone could discern a single aspect of that "other me"

from the way I smoke. I may, in fact, puff in the same way I always did, but what, after all, is significant about that? I thought that they all went on about Bette Davis and the smoking — not me. Recognizing me from my smoking style is impossible — partially because my arms don't work with the fluidity that they once did.

And then there is my posture — but you needn't be reminded of that. I keep forgetting that my physical presence doesn't horrify you. You are simply not here. You do not try to escape me, as so many do these days, because of my horrific outer self. I think it is because I am beyond surgery. Everyone knows that the old still secretly exist, but when they appear in public, no one knows that they are old. When did age become obscenity? It was gradually becoming obscene when Dash was trying to write his thesis about Shakespeare.

I went out the other day to buy cigarettes. They now cost a week's wages — one thousand dollars a pack. Can you imagine spending a week of a rich man's wages for a mere twenty-five cigarettes? And I decided, because, after all, I still do enjoy making a scene, that I would not use the wheelchair. When I'm in my wheelchair, people can't tell where the machine ends and I begin. I am robot; and in this way I am picturesque. I fit in; I am a part of the modern world. There is the hint of a living person there somewhere, but the image of the machine overwhelms and transforms me into a somewhat comforting vision.

Instead, I used the cane. Yes, *the cane.* This means I was walking — if you can call it that — at a snail's pace. And of course you know my eternal posture these days is an "L" shape: that is how my body has formed itself. This is very tragic for others to see. But the worst part, the part I hate, is that they actually curse me; they want me to die. When they are behind me — if for some reason they can't get around me — they say in a voice I can clearly hear: "For fuck's sake, hurry up!" Once someone said, absolutely audibly: "Do you think you could go any slower?" We live in an eternity of nothingness; the applause is all around us in cyberspace. We all have many, many friends we may speak to and see pictures of — but how are we sure it is really them? Because of the wonderful implants they've given us, we are suddenly "integrated." We are beautiful forever in cyberspace. And so my obscene infirmity is more than an abutment, more than an obstruction or a rebellion: it is a slap — no, a gunshot to the gut.

After purchasing the cigarettes, I very slowly made my way home. The corner store is one of the few remaining reminders of the way we once were. They should be banned. There, people once fell in love; dogs sniffed each other; etc. Back then, there was the "Internet" too, and people could imagine they were romancing the person at the next table. Zing went the strings. (There, I said it. So what?) One of the most fascinating things about contemporary culture is that these corner stores are owned by Walmart and Walmart has designed them to seem like the corner stores of the past. They've researched every detail, even hired non-white faces to work in them, and jacked up the prices so we can have that strange comforting guilt of tucking away a package of cookies at twice the price for the convenience of picking them up conveniently.

I arrived home with my thousand-dollar cigarettes and I savoured one — which cost me, what was it, approximately fifty bucks? I anticipated you railing against my new lifestyle, against the possibility that I might go back there. I won't. How could I? It would mean death, of course. And the strange pile of papers and their scribblings? Oh, we will get to more of the scribblings the next time we talk. I do love you most when you are very angry at me. I am the decrepit, crumbling child; like one of those dwarfish tragic, chinless, bespectacled children who age too early, I have gone beyond my "in-between" status. (Remember when I sang that song? Of course you do.) I have moved far beyond Andy Hardy. The joy of unconditional love is that no test is too great, and there are no final threats. Is this true? (Don't answer, please, don't answer, my darling, please.) I love you.

I am still reeling from your last letter. I can almost smell the invective. I read and reread the first few paragraphs. I think what I treasure most are your threats. All this talk about my liver — can you not see that it is old-fashioned? As you well know, they have made a fourth from my own tissue; it is therefore inde-structible — or so they tell me.

I think this was the turning point for civilization, if I may digress. But I want you to know that what you have said is serious, very serious, and your threats are real. I do acknowledge that. I want you to think about the time when there was some sense — an order that was more than random — when we had to take threats to our health seri-ously. Do you remember when there were consequences? When actions had results? There was a time when med-ical insurance cost more if you put your life in danger, and people thought about taking risks in terms of the cost of their health insurance. Do you remember? Without laser healing, regenerative organ replacement and cyberbodies, these things had to be taken into account. The turning point came when people began to believe there *were no consequences*. Remember the middle of the last century, when doctors had a smoke while they warned you of the dangers of lung cancer? It seems we have returned to that era. One day people stopped caring about what they did, and ethics became inconsequential. Ethics are related to survival, but when survival is taken care of in ways that we don't entirely understand, ethics become a questionable luxury. Fortunately we have the police. *Un*fortunately, the police can do nothing about hurt, betrayal, insensitivity or lies. No there are no personal penalties either — little that's left is personal.

There is one thing about Dash's essay that I particularly liked. Dash talks about Olivier's Hamlet giving up, giving himself over to death and flying like a bird — with his sword drawn — and finally falling on Claudius and killing him. He reads Hamlet not as a destroyer, but as a mystic. One who surrenders himself to the death instinct. Isn't that what we've all done? We have given up, and why shouldn't we? It is the only response. We know things will be taken care of, that things will be done for us, and that someone (we are not entirely sure who) is in charge. There is something unhuman, or dis-human, but completely typical and human about this response. On the one hand, Aristotle imagined that being human involved action, decision. But then the philosophies of the Far East — and, it seems, Hamlet — were telling us the opposite: that to be human is to relinquish all claims to the ability to change our fate. The concept of fate itself is old-fashioned. Fate still implies fighting *against* something: "Do not go gentle . . ." Of course, I gave up long ago. (Thank God.)

Now, to address your concerns, because yes, they must be addressed. So I will calmly sit and mouth the words *my father*. I was astounded when you made reference to him, but I have every right to respond in kind, now that you have thrown down the gauntlet. And I know what you expect — you expect me to stop. You expect that the spectre of *all that* will be enough to shut me up. I'm not sure that it is.

I *will* talk about him, and I will say that I blame it all on the ushers — one in particular. His name was Francisco. Frank, for short. I am not saying my father didn't experience desire for the ushers, but I don't believe his lust was ever consummated. It was a different era. Do you understand what it was like to be the manager of a movie theatre back then? He was a member of a Showmen's League, of course. He was a showman and a performer. But back then running a movie theatre was more than just hiring projectionists. When he started, there were vaudeville acts between the films. Nowadays we know only the megatheatres we create for ourselves in our heads, the cyberexperience of going to the theatre.

It's my fault if I *go back there*, as you kept repeating, over and over. I can't believe you use that phrase, as if I could actually go back in time! How can I convince you? It's gone! I am not *her*. My body is desiccated; I've come to terms with it, and so can you. But those ushers were fucking beautiful. And people who are beautiful and know it just don't understand those who aren't and don't.

There are two different kinds of people in this world; there is simply a dividing line and never, never, shall the twain meet. Yes, Mayer called me his "little hunchback." But look what I have become! He was right, of course. I'm more than a hunchback: I am the Hunchback of Notre Dame. But it wasn't about what I looked like, it was never that. And it has nothing to do with anorexia. I wasn't anorexic — a disease that causes you not to see your real body at all. Anorexia is about control — about controlling life and death. That is not relevant to my case. I just hated the way I looked. And Louis B. could call me whatever he wanted, and men could ejaculate all over me — many did. But it didn't matter, because I never believed, I never once believed, for one second, that I was beautiful. I was never connected to my body. But I knew that beauty was the most important thing. And I knew there were people like that, people who were connected to their bodies in a fundamental way. They didn't have to learn how to love their bodies, or how to be attractive. They just *were*.

When I think of the ushers around my father, I think of how they tortured him. My father, like me, always hated his body, didn't understand it, would have been better off without it. But Francisco and the other ushers were different. They were all dark boys, for some reason. They were probably Hispanics — it was southern California. My father would take me to the theatre and introduce me to them, and they would swarm around him like flowers showing their faces to the sun — and they'd touch him! I saw them touch him. I'm not fucking saying that if my father molested them, it wasn't his fault. But he didn't! I'm sure he didn't. Sure he wanted them, he wanted *it* so badly — and it wasn't just because he was a homosexual. Who would *not* fucking want them?

You know very well about those who used be called "straight" men — the men who have sex with women — how proud they once were about *not* being attracted to other men. But how can anyone *not* be attracted to men? Oh Christ, how I hate those women who go on and on about how they don't have "those kinds of desires" — we all know what that means. It's all about the penis being ugly. June Allyson was like that. Sure, I loved her onscreen. Who wouldn't love her, if for no reason other than that *voice*, and what happened to it. She was a very nice person — but nice only goes so far, you know? There was a "butter wouldn't melt in her mouth" thing going on with her.

I think there are two kinds of women. The cocksuckers and the . . . not. The not *are* women who just couldn't be bothered to do that unpleasant thing to their husbands — as they are, invariably, married. Well, what's the problem? I would even argue that there is still an identity politics — but it has nothing to do with object choice. It has to do with whether or not you are a cocksucker. I know you've sucked the odd cock. And I know you're not fond of it. But it's not like you'd go on about it, scrunch up your eyes — that's what June Allyson would do, scrunch up her eyes, become girlish and revulsed: "Ew! How could anyone *do* that?" I don't know how to tell you, June — thanks a lot for the sentiment, but there's nothing quite like managing to get a thick one down your throat. And if you can't grovel — I mean, really get down and grovel — in front of a dick, then you haven't lived, and you don't know nuthin', baby.

Now, that doesn't mean I devalue clits. But if we're talking about genital ugliness here, who wins the prize? In the last analysis, the wrinkles of a scrotum and the folds of labia are in a dead heat. You're bound to be repulsed by one or the other — but to be repulsed by both? There's something seriously wrong with you.

I think it has to do with humility and the human condition, because it's all about ugliness. This is what I don't understand, and what makes me feel really old. Ugliness used to be the big secret for anybody who liked to whore around. Nowadays no one is allowed to be ugly, so we've forgotten how to get off on it. But people left to their own devices are drawn to ugliness. Not because they're settling, or because they can't get that special cute one, but just because ugly is fucking sexy, and grovelling in front of it is sexy. And that's what it's all about. It's where sex and death come together, if you want to get philosophical. But at this moment, frankly, I don't.

But back to the ushers that used to swarm around my father. They weren't ugly, but they knew that what they had between their legs was ugly. And they knew that he wanted it. As I've said, why wouldn't he? He was human. But they also knew he hated himself for it. My mother was one of the June Allysons, one of the face scrunchers. "Put that away, that's ugly." I'm sure she said that to my father. I know it must have happened in the dark for them to beget three kids — they probably drilled a hole in a sheet like the Mormons and the Jews and the you-know-who-we-aren't-allowed-to-mention. Yes, I'm going to say that — *I'm going to say that*. I mean, who is actually listening? Everybody and nobody, as I understand it — whatever that means. I know how careful everyone is, but I don't feel like being that fucking paranoid.

Just think about this tortured man. He knows the kind of ugliness he wants, and he goes to work, and those ushers swarm around him. . . . If you want to know the truth, he fired Francisco. Why? Because Francisco came on to him, and he was afraid he might give in to the temptation. That's what happened. And then two weeks later Francisco was reporting him to the police. I know all this because my mother told us. I mean, she didn't tell us in so many words. But she told us in enough words that we would grow up being seriously conflicted about our father.

But Jesus, I couldn't hate him. I knew I was supposed to; I knew she wanted me to hate him, but I didn't. If I thought my father had ever forced anybody to do anything sexual with him, I would never defend him, not for one second — I would want to rip his guts out. He was just one of those tortured guys. And there were so many of them who never did anything except on the sly, in the dark, with someone else who wanted it, someone who wanted it more than he did, and who suffered in silence. But when those weedy flowers with the pretty faces would start pressing against him, he would get crazy and do anything to get away.

And that's all I'm going to say.

I'm also not going to talk about the radio show. Okay? If you want me to go *there*, just throw down that gauntlet again. But I will say this: my father and I were a lot alike.

However, I'm not my father. I'd be dead by now if I was.

It's you who is misinterpreting my scholarship. You are twisting everything around. And suddenly Dash King becomes my father, and I'm my father, and pretty well everyone is my father! Untrue. Because when it came down to it, you know I was pretty insulted when they tried to say that my "affection for homosexuals" had something to do with him. It didn't. I *was* a homosexual, as far as I was concerned. I mean, that's pretty fucking clear.

And don't listen to Liza, please don't listen to what she said. You know I don't like trashing my own children, I really don't, but she whitewashed things. She liked to paint a pretty picture. Not sure why, not sure who that serves in the end. "Mama was a good person." Yeah, well, good *intentions* . . . maybe. "Mama took care of us." Well, no. I mean, I was there until they grew up, I didn't abandon them. And I supported them financially because that was the easy part — until it got hard. But a good mother doesn't get taken care of by her children. She takes care of them. I can't tell you how that must have fucked them up.

Look, I'm interested in Dash King, not because he is what used to be called a homosexual — like my father. I'm a scholar now, remember? I'm interested in the decline of the West. And part of that decline is not, as so many assume, due to the ascendance of homosexuality, but instead to the disappearance of it. Orgies are not about desire. When people get all horned up, they normally don't have orgies, they don't obliterate themselves with sex. Orgies are all about repression and self-hatred. Orgies and decadence are the symptoms of a civilization that is struggling with repression. Sex and sexuality do not have a natural inclination to get out of hand (as Freud suggested) — no pun intended. The tendency of sex is not towards too much sex, it's just toward, perhaps, more sex. Too much sex is something that happens when people are afraid they might not ever have sex again.

Dash was writing during a period when people were witnessing the end of sex. Sex was virtually over, in the sense that virtual sex had taken over what used to be called sex. It wasn't just that people began to live in the virtual world — though they did. It's that the virtual world became so available to them that there was no longer any way for them to measure or understand their real lives. It started in my era; I was one of the causes. (But I didn't write the movies, so please don't blame me.) It was because of Hollywood that millions of people — especially women — grew up imagining that love had something to do with sunsets, violins, perfect profiles and happily ever afters. Not having lived through this, you cannot imagine what it was like. And this deluded rush after an ever-dwindling perfect was the media's fault.

But the movies had nothing on pornography. It was one thing to destroy love. But to destroy sex — that really gets people where they live. I mean that in the sense that one of the few links we have to reality has now disappeared. Sex used to be, if nothing else, real. You have written about the state of current sexuality — and the state of the university life. But as one who actually lived through it all — amazingly — I have a unique perspective.

I'm only mentioning this to re-emphasize the context for Dash's sad obsessions. He was writing passionately, and he was disintegrating, at the end of the era when sex was still real. That he never obtained the precious title of Doctor might be tragic — if the title had not become so meaningless. That I am a Doctor and you are a Doctor has, of course, more to do with the fact that we have somehow been able to satisfy the various corporations that now go under the name of universities. In Dash's time, academia had not quite reached that stage of decadence. It's important to note that these were once at least semi-real institutes of learning. There was a very earnest pursuit of research, and some accent was actually placed on teaching. However, it's true that even in Dash's time this was all changing. The obsession with technology would eventually lead to our present situation — the cold, soulless efficiency of virtual classrooms in which human teachers have become obsolete. It's so easy to forget that the beginning of the millennium was still, to some degree, in the shadow of the sixties; that there was still a notion of academic freedom — even though universities were gradually receiving less and less funding from the government and beginning to work in the service of business. Today it behooves us to justify the pragmatism of everything we do; back then this was only just starting to occur. I have you to thank, as usual, for the fact that I can research pretty well anything I desire. But your well-inflected but dangerous implication — I was surprised that you dared — that I was a very famous person hiding in secret (in the secrecy of an unrecognizable body, in fact!) was enough to subsidize a fat salary for me until I die. (If I ever die.) Nothing interests a university more these days than the possibility that one of its professors might become a cybercelebrity. But aren't we all cybercelebrities?

Back then it was much the same, in terms of academia. Dash got his position as a rather elderly graduate student because he had some experience in the "gay theatre." His name had been in the newspapers (remember how important the newspapers once were?) for founding a gay theatre in Toronto. At the turn of the century, we find Dash desperate for work. He has been turned out of the theatre he founded. The cause? A lessening interest in identity politics, and a general abandonment of experimental and political work by both artists and funding bodies. The sad part is that Dash could never come to terms with what had happened to him.

Now, of course, we understand that old people are just that — old. As soon as their bodies begin to be replaced by the necessary machinery, it is time for them to be seen as rarely as possible and certainly never heard. At that time there was still a romantic notion that age might be meaningless. I remember eagerly watching romance movies during the sixties. Older women fell for younger men or vice versa, and the precious *de rigueur* lines of the era included the ubiquitous "age means nothing to me." The irony today is that the old still have sex with the young, or try to. But when the young perceive that a potential partner may be somewhat cyborgian, they reject them. When people look into each other's eyes these days, they are trying to detect laser eye surgery, and will summarily abandon their potential partner if there is even the hint of a cataract. I'm sure you've heard that some young people actually carry metal-detection devices to root out the more ancient suitors.

But when Dash was fired from his little gay Toronto theatre, he was in his early fifties. And though life had clearly passed him by — that is, his creative and romantic life was effectively over — he was valiantly and pathetically trying to jump-start a second career to remain young. I know this because he wrote several articles that are still easily findable, articles that deal with aging. In these articles he babbles bathetically about what a good time can be had by older homosexuals. He claims they are still desirable, they are misrepresented in the media, they are misunderstood as "garden variety fags." This last was his invented terminology for older conservative gay men — fags who garden. You really should look up these old identity-based articles, they're quite a hoot.

Dash King's plays are also an entertainment in themselves. He wrote quickly, so quickly that it was impossible for him ever to write a great play (or what might be considered great by the artistic standards of the time). Some of his plays were written in the space of one week, and he often defended himself by comparing himself to the likes of Donizetti, Noël Coward and Lope de Vega. We won't even discuss Donizetti and Lope de Vega; they were prolific, but that is something quite different than shallow and careless. As for Noël Coward, not even Noël Coward ever lived up to being Noël Coward, and if *Private Lives was* written in a week, it certainly shows. Some of Dash King's plays can still be found, and there is something touching about them. But more as an antithesis to the "Death of the Author" paradigm: they are interesting only because of what one knows about the author. I think Mr. King would have been quite perturbed to know that he has not been remembered, not even as a gay activist. In fact, one of his whining articles goes on about his concern that he will be remembered as a gay activist rather than as an artist. Well, the fact is, the only chance he has of being remembered at all is if our discussion of his lost papers becomes the foundation for an article that is widely read. This is, in itself, also unlikely. Anyway, the plays are mostly unreadable rants about homosexuality, peppered with nostalgia for the good old days of gay liberation when gay men were girls and had "high heels in their hearts" — one of my favourite kitschy

King lines. As I say, the plays hold little interest except as a footnote to his tragic life.

His imploded scholarship, however — especially the scribbled notes on several printed versions of the *Hamlet* essay — is interesting, particularly in the context of his heroic attempt to resurrect identity politics at a time when they were so very clearly over. I neglected to mention the *Hamlet* article marginalia because I am saving the best for last. King's essay appeared in an online journal when online scholarship was in its infancy. The journal was concerned with the notion that Shakespeare was not "the man from Stratford," as the journal likes to put it, but instead Edward de Vere, the Earl of Oxford.

There were many reasons why a late-twentieth-century faction who called themselves "Oxfordians" had decided that the Earl of Oxford was the real Shakespeare. But for King it was all a matter of identity politics — everything was. Other heterosexually identified Oxfordians found the proof they needed for identifying de Vere as Shakespeare in the Earl's background, life and learning. He was an aristocrat, and was certainly a very learned — if not a dissipated, and perhaps criminal — sort of man. When one begins to research the old Oxfordian websites, one may be surprised by the notion that their entertaining fictions might indeed be fact. There are certainly a remarkable series of coincidences connecting the two men. For instance, the Earl's life resembles, to a shocking degree, the plots of Shakespeare's plays. The Earl of Oxford had three daughters, was married to a woman who cuckolded him (or was thought to), spent much time in Europe, was the adopted nephew of the real-life person on whom Polonius was inarguably based . . . The list of coincidental similarities goes on and on. All of this might matter — if Shakespeare mattered. It might matter if work that is so antique and indecipherable was still read or performed; if it still interested people in any way other than in an archaeological sense.

For King, who considered himself a playwright, Shakespeare was a romantic figure. The mystery surrounding his identity became an obsession. King's interest was related to the fact that de Vere was probably a sodomite, in an Early Modern sense: that is, he probably had sex with boys. He had brought from his Italian travels a castrato with whom he was rumoured to have been intimate. King's argument in his essay is for an effeminate Hamlet: that Hamlet is a difficult character to portray because he is effeminate — and therefore, according to a Foucauldian definition of sexuality, gay. King is suggesting that Stratfordians (i.e., Nelson, below) argue that de Vere could not have been Shakespeare because he was an effeminate sodomite. King wants to celebrate Hamlet, and de Vere's sexuality, and claim them, essentially, as homosexuals. In the key passage, he begins in classical identity politics style, criticizing Nelson (de Vere's poisonous, Stratfordian biographer) for being homophobic:

> Particularly interesting is Nelson's focus on what he obviously perceives as one of Oxford's most significant character flaws: his alleged propensity for buggery. One of the chapters in Nelson's biography is labelled "Sodomite," and in his introduction Nelson finds fault with one of the earliest and most prominent Oxfordians, Bernard M. Ward. Nelson suggests that in Ward's Oxfordian (and therefore slanted) biography of Oxford, "solid information is thus suppressed in the interest of good form, and also, in Ward's case, to protect Oxford's reputation."[3] What "solid information"? For example, Nelson suggests Oxford's enemies

accused him of being a sodomite but "where anyone who casts half an eye over the libel manuscripts in the PRO [Public Record Office] will encounter the words 'sodomy' and 'buggery,' Ward retreats into circumlocution."[4] Nelson's biography takes two questionable assumptions for granted — first, that a great artist must necessarily be a "good" person, and second, that homosexuality is a flaw that is unlikely to be found in a man whom many consider to be the greatest poet of all time.

The attached notes to this passage show that even at this time of supposed academic freedom, King had to deal with censorship around what were then issues of sexuality. This hurt and angered him deeply. You see, as eager as the "Oxfordians" were to prove that de Vere was Shakespeare, they were also eager to protect de Vere's reputation. King is astute enough to focus his article not just on Shakespeare's sexuality, but on whether or not the greatest writer of all time was — or had to be — a "good" person. But the two go hand in hand: an evil Shakespeare would be one who was profligate, homosexual — and a good one would be, presumably, happily married and monogamous, or perhaps even celibate. So, attached to the above passage, on three separate sheets of paper, are three alternative versions of the last sentences of the above paragraph from King's essay. King saved them, in melancholy fashion, to prove a point to his advisor.

All of these papers appear to be addressed to Antonio Legato, an elderly University of Toronto professor emeritus. (There are no comments from Legato in King's papers, but Dr. Legato is sometimes addressed in the papers.) At any rate, it is in the following three versions of the same paragraph that we come to see the disintegration of King's scholarship (or his attempt at scholarship) and its implications. It matters little to the academic community that King became disillusioned. Yet I find it fascinating. In these papers we read King's private agony over the censorship he perceived had been directed against him. And it seems pretty clear from the paragraphs below that, indeed, he had been censored. The first paragraph is labelled "Additions by the editor." The paragraph begins where the passage above ends, and we can see that after "the greatest poet of all time," a parenthetical passage has been added, for obvious reasons:

> Nelson's biography takes two questionable assumptions for granted — first, that a great artist must necessarily be a "good" person, and second, that homosexuality is a flaw that is unlikely to be found in a man whom many consider to be the greatest poet of all time. (Now, de Vere was undoubtedly heterosexual — he had the children and family to prove it.)

What is evident is that because a squeamish Oxfordian journal did not want to see the Earl of Oxford (their candidate for Shakespeare) presented as a homosexual, they added a parenthetical sentence informing us that the Earl of Oxford was not gay. The next attached passage is labelled by King as what was finally printed. We see now that the paragraph is longer still, with further additions:

> Nelson's biography takes two questionable assumptions for granted — first, that a great artist must necessarily be a "good" person, and second, that homosexuality is a flaw that is unlikely to be found in a man whom many consider to be

the greatest poet of all time. Now, de Vere was undoubtedly heterosexual — he had the children and family to prove it. Also, he was a confirmed "man's man," being an enormously successful warrior who served many times on the field of battle, and had the battle scars to prove it.

King's anguished note, following these passages, I find heart-wrenching:

Antonio:
I called Balthazar Goetz and had the most horrible conversation with him. He seemed like such a nice man via email. I suppose he is nice; he just has no idea what I'm talking about. I said, "Dr. Goetz, what about the changes to my article?" Of course, there was nothing I could do about it. I had allowed the smaller changes because they twisted my arm (are journals supposed to do that?). But when I saw they printed all that stuff about Oxford being a "man's man," I was at my wit's end. At first Dr. Goetz claimed ignorance, saying I had given him permission. Well, yes, I had given him permission to say that Oxford was married and had two children, because that happens to be true. (Even though it doesn't prove anything about his sexuality.) But I was not warned about all the inserted sentences suggesting Oxford was masculine. And this is supposed to prove that he was straight? Dr. Goetz said, "Didn't we run that by you?" I told him that he hadn't. He apologized and said, "But doesn't it make sense?" What am I supposed to say to that? I tried to get him to understand the basic Butlerian difference between

a performed gender identity and sexual orientation. I also tried to make him understand that it is very important for me to open up the possibility that de Vere was a homosexual. The saddest part is that he doesn't seem to have read his Butler or to even care about the issue. "But de Vere always won at his jousting tournaments. Doesn't that suggest he was a man's man?" Can you imagine? He seemed like a very nice person . . . who didn't give a damn about sexual politics. It wouldn't be so bad if his attitude wasn't the general attitude, and if his answer hadn't made me feel so small. And so alone. I'm sorry to get so personal. But what's happened here seems like a turning point to me.

Another letter is beneath this one:

Antonio:
One more thing.

I don't understand why they couldn't simply leave my writing alone. Why was it so important to make the point that the Earl of Oxford was *not* gay? The whole argument I am trying to make in this article is that Oxford may be gay, and Hamlet may be effeminate (and therefore meant to be read as gay), but those things shouldn't make us respect him any less. We should be able to love Hamlet and Edward de Vere — and Shakespeare, for that matter — even if they were all gay. And what about de Vere's Italian castrato? But I guess he didn't have testicles after all — so was he ever really a man or even a boy? The final edit was done completely without my permission. I don't know what to do. I can't pull the article once it's published. As I said, I am at my wit's end. I honestly don't see how I can ever be a scholar.

This little mishap (at one point Goetz actually called it both "little" and "a mishap") makes me feel *so* depressed. I know I am not supposed to take any of this personally. That's not what it's all about. Maybe I am too "dramatic" to be an academic. Call me crazy, but my sexuality is important to me, and I think Shakespeare's sexuality should be important to everyone. Of course, I might be making such a fuss about this because I know, somewhere, in my heart of hearts, that the reason I was summarily booted out of my theatre company was because of identity politics. I had created a little space for myself where I thought I might still be able to write about the issues that are important to me. I am now feeling quite manic about this; and I know I'm not even supposed to *have* feelings about an essay. I'll tell you something: heterosexuals just don't get it. They just don't get what it means to be gay, and they never will, and I'm beginning to think there's just no point trying to tell them. And if that's true, then there's no point in me writing anymore, there's no point in me creating anything.

I know this letter is becoming very unacademic. I have spoken to my partner about this. As you know, he is much younger than me; much, much younger. I can't believe it, but he seems to have rejected identity politics too. "Why do you care whether or not Shakespeare is gay? Who cares about Shakespeare?" he said. I've finally realized that there is a huge gulf between us. When I met Jason he was in his late twenties and of course very attractive and there was something of the seventies of gay liberation about him. He understood my politics, he understood the importance of creating a gay culture. Now he too seems to have, in principle at least, rejected the whole gay sensibility, and the importance of writing about gay culture. "I kinda think gay is over," he said. I can't believe that a contested line in an essay would cause me so much pain; I don't know what to do. Right now I want to quit everything, and I mean *everything*. You've been so supportive up until now; I hope this note doesn't just drive you away. But I had to *try* to share it with somebody. Ignore this letter if you wish. I know I have gone over some boundaries here; you are, after all, not my therapist; you are my thesis advisor — and there's a big difference.

— Dash

And that's it. The letters become more pitiful from there. King continues to vent to Legato. And Legato — who was very open-minded in his heyday, a prototypical university radical of the sixties — can do nothing but try to be King's analyst. Why did he bother? Partially just because Legato was a nice old man. But it was also true that Dash was a bit of a commodity at the time, an art star that the University of Toronto wanted to keep around at all costs.

I understand if you don't want me to speak another word about Dash King's papers. Just because it's my area of interest doesn't mean it will be yours. Is it possible, now that I've shown you more of Dash's writing and explained my interest, that the whole thing might make sense? That maybe you'll stop attacking and threatening? To be honest, all of this has made me think about two things: my father in a shack, and . . . playing a moonbeam. I'll tell you more about that later if you are willing to listen.

You looked directly into my eyes once and said, "I will never leave you alone." And then you left for London. I understand why, and of course I do forgive you. I love you so much and I know that truly leaving me would mean . . . I wouldn't be able to communicate with you anymore.

I am willing to risk that.

By being honest.

I don't know how I feel about psychoanalysis. I've had a lot of it, and it seems the more I have, the less I like it. A good psychiatrist ends up teaching you how little you need him. And so it's pretty clear to me what you're trying to do and it won't work.

If, as you say, I am teetering on some sort of edge, then does challenging my identity sound like a good idea? I think I may need to see you in person. If my new academic focus is going to end our friendship, the least you can do is come to Toronto and say goodbye. I know you have (or had) a friend here. We won't go into that. I know we mustn't. But surely you could risk seeing her if it meant seeing me. If you don't want to risk coming here to say goodbye — which is the least you could do — then I am, to quote Mr. King, "at my wit's end." I know you take issue with King's fondness for homosexual hyperbole. I should not even quote him, and certainly should not imitate his diction.

So yes, the fact is — at the very least — you find my academic interests shallow. And you think the entire pur-suit of this worthless and perhaps unsavoury subject is wrong. No, more than wrong — a catastrophe waiting to happen. I have lost my mind, or I am losing my mind, according to you. The fact that I have a cigarette now and then is enough to start you raving. You think it's not about King at all. You think I couldn't care less about King. And anyway, it's all a ruse. Ultimately, you believe I shouldn't care about him because he is a typical, shallow homosexual. I am going to go back, certain to return forever to the dark days. This temptation is an indication, a warning signal, a dire, dangerous turning point.

You really are a very serious person. And I am not. Even though I pretend to be. What I mean is that I am essentially an optimist, while you love dread, revel in it. Nothing could be more exciting for you than imagining the most severe of outcomes. I sometimes think that if there were no horrific consequences, there would be no point to living for you at all.

So it may just be that we have different ways of looking at things. For me this new academic subject matter is simply a risky change, a refreshing new leaf: "Open a new window; open a new door!" (If I hadn't had to get a second new liver, I could have played that part in the movie!) For you it's something akin to swallowing a busload of pills and inviting strangers to my hotel room for blow jobs. But then, perhaps I am not the only one who is not in her right mind. Maybe what I have said has also triggered you. I know that when you were young you nursed several old homosexuals who were dying of AIDS. (Amazing that they can cure so much today, but not that, hmmm....) And perhaps you had a bit too much of that kind of self-destruction. Those old homosexuals didn't like to call it that, but of course what else was going on? In fact, when they began to take care of their health, have safe sex and slow down a bit on the non-pharmaceuticals, they got better.

At any rate, you don't want to be my friend and/or mentor if I am going to be self-destructive, do you? But I'm going to accuse you of what you are accusing me. In other words, your reaction to my "subject matter" is not as unemotional and measured as you think it appears. Instead, it shows evidence of panicked emotional baggage. But whatever is actually going on between us — and I'm sure one way or another we will find out — I must directly address your analysis of my situation. For you know very well what you are doing. It's not been that long since I've seen you.

And besides, I will never forget what it was like to watch you sitting across from me, preparing to chastise me. I can picture your face, warming up to the challenge. You get that irritated, angry look in your eyes. You imagine I'm going to have a fit and start crying — and then you won't get to say everything you want to say. And so you push the vituperation, ratchet up the attack. All this because you have to test me — make sure I'm not going to run and cry, descend into my old, childish, self-destroying self.

I am here to tell you I am a changed woman. Or, more accurately, a changed being. I welcome criticism — I do. I know you don't believe me. I am quite cool, calm and collected — despite the ancient crippled pile of bones I appear to be. I am also fully capable of leading a counterattack.

You raise a particularly cutting critique of Dash King's letters — the notion that they are shallow. It's important for us to address this because it is the typical reaction one finds to homosexual writing of any sort. To some degree, it's Wilde's fault, because he went on about the lie that tells the truth, the mask being more honest than the face beneath, and style being more important than substance. (You will see later that Dash, too, is concerned with the notion of style and substance.) Eve Sedgwick, bless her heart, suggested that the lie of Modernism was that an obsession with style was meant to hide the desire for a beautiful young man's body. She meant that a beautiful young man's body was the content of Wilde's contentless works of art. A lovely notion, prettily expressed. In other words, whenever Modernists go on about the amorality of art and aesthetics, they are actually talking about a very large penis — the elephant in the room whose tumescence fills the vacuum left by empty Modernism. For instance, Wilde claimed *The Picture of Dorian Gray* was not about anything; it was amoral. In the introduction to his play he goes on and on about "true art." "True art" has no moral; it is simply beautiful. But his novel actually concerns itself with a very specific beauty, that of a young man. Wilde would rather that we didn't notice.

But all this is too easy. It's too easy to dismiss Wilde for the things he celebrated in himself. To call Oscar Wilde shallow would be like calling Michael Jackson showbizzy, Beau Brummell vain or Donald Trump (remember him?) rich. Of course Wilde was shallow, but only in the sense that he suggested that the shallowest things were actually the deepest. This means his constant ranting against naturalism was a bit of a pose. (Like everything he did.) Wilde believed naturalism was shallow. But it *was* only shallow, and not paradoxically deep. Naturalism was simply bad writing. Wilde was quite right to scorn it and to try to create beauty beyond the ordinary. *The Importance of Being Earnest* is about the rhythm and the fascination of completely trivial things: vanity, lechery, greed and hypocrisy. And yet, these things are not trivial at all.

What I'm trying to say is that to call a homosexual shallow — or the homosexual movement, or homosexuals in general — is in itself shallow. It is playing into their hand, and their hand is, more often than not, holding their own — or someone else's — cock.

So do you really want to go there?

But it's more than that. Because at the basis of everything you're saying is something we have to confront now or never.

When we first met, one of the things that brought us together was homosexuality. Of course, there were no bona fide homosexuals left, but we were women who enjoyed the concept of homosexuality, and occasionally had had sex with men who would have been called "queers" at an earlier time. (Me much more than you, of course.) There is a kind of imaginary world going on here. You — who pride yourself on seeing beyond the myth of what we used to call "the Fantasy Me" — are caught in the web of its fiction, terribly insecure about me becoming immersed in it all again. Of course, there were individual homosexuals with whom I became entangled. And there was Mickey. (Not Rooney. Of course, you know which Mickey I mean. But that's different.)

Okay, let me say it once and for all.

I didn't like them. I didn't like *it*. (By it, I mean the whole "homosexual as my audience" thing.) I wasn't *in love* with them. I didn't *do it all* for them. I didn't *play it for the homosexuals*. And this is the most important idea of all — *they didn't kill me*. And by that, I don't mean simply the tautology that I am not dead. Or, at least, I don't think I am. And I imagine I can be trusted in these matters. Or are we going to throw out Descartes with the bathwater?

What I mean is that I died in a very public way — though I actually continued living. And the homosexuals were thought to be responsible for my death. They loved me too much; they had showered me with too much applause — they fed my soul-crushing need for drugs by pressing me back onstage night after night to fulfill their extravagant demands for entertainment. They created "the

Fantasy Me," "the Unreal Me" and ultimately "the Dead Me." The homosexuals become — as the French were once to the English (or the Turks and Greeks to almost everyone in Western Europe) — the abject purveyors of an evil influence. Everything they touch turns to dross — no, to shit — and dies.

This is all just homophobia, ancient and cloying.

No, they did not kill me; they did not curse me, love me too much or contaminate me with their love. The whole idea is ridiculous. Don't get me wrong, I knew they were there. For one thing, they were always in the front row. It makes me sad to think about them. But it's not nostalgia; it's more piquant. I was, to them, something panting, untouchable, inexplicable — so near yet so very far, a rare tropical dying bird, something religious, a mystic vision. It's too much to say I was their mother. I think a lot of them had fine mothers. Have you ever met a mother of a homosexual? She's like anyone's mother, the same infuriating mixture of saint and monster. But homosexuals are no more obsessed with their mothers than we are. They may have talked about them and written about them more, but that's just because so many of them were writers.

But the front row, it would inevitably be natty young men in thin ties and very expensive Arrow shirts. And I want you to think for a moment. How could I *not* be conscious of what was going on? When I played those concerts for them, I was desperately in need of money to keep the kids by my side. And I was doing what I always did. I was performing the best I could, goddamn it. But it wasn't for them; it was for me. Do you know what I thought about when I looked at them — rigid, intense, frozen, asphyxiated with adoration?

I pitied them.

Not for loving my work — they were moved by me,

that's fine; that's what I get the rush from. I'm talking about the cult of *me*, the worship of *me*, I'm talking about the political party that I didn't even ask to be the president of, that I wouldn't ever wish to preside over. I'm talking about people who — instead of living their own lives — were competing to touch my hand. Some made their homes shrines to me and didn't eat, didn't sleep, didn't fuck (most pitiful of all) because of me. They were lost little boys. They were not lost because they were homosexuals. They were lost because homosexuality at the time meant being excluded from the most aristocratic of artistic professions. These were the florists, the interior decorators, the hairdressers, the chorus boys — forever, they thought, relegated to the subsidiary arts. No one else would hire them, because they were freaks. They were lisping, effeminate, outcast ninnies.

I wish I could say I loved them. I loved performing for anyone who would really listen. And many of them did. But that's as far as it went. I watched my funeral on TV. Of course, you already know that; I told you about it. But I don't think I ever told you the extent of my disgust, which was realized, in practical form, by my laughter. It was very cruel laughter — what can I say, I'm not going to apologize. I had a good laugh. Who were these freaks? And I don't mean their effeminacy. How many prancing girlettes placed wreathes on my coffin, and knelt down to kiss it, one pinky raised in the air, their painted eyelashes damp with tears? Don't get me wrong, I'm sorry their lives were so harsh. But their much-vaunted love for me was all about a human impulse I've never really understood — the stupid, desperate (and this is the worst part), unimaginative need to be a part of a pack, a herd — to be, once and for all, accepted.

People always natter on about how I wanted love.

All she wanted was love. And the homosexuals gave it to her. And that love killed her.

Fuck off.

I was a fucking artist and I knew what I was doing. I was damn good at it, even when I was fucking lousy. And I always gave them a show; I always gave everybody a fucking show, not just those crazy homosexuals.

And later? Later it was much worse. I mean, back in the day, I didn't have contempt for them really — or tried not to. But after my "death," they continued to buy my records and it went beyond beyond. Don't get me wrong, the records are okay. But I really was a live performer, a living performer. You had to see me live. And here they were collecting my records and gossiping about my demise. Here they were enjoying interviews in which I'm drunk or clearly on drugs (and there were many such instances). And they only did this because they wanted to *belong*. I was a drunken light-house, a shot in the dark, the delirious painted-pony mascot they hoped would lead them out of their social insecurities.

I don't think that later, in the seventies and eighties, when the drag queens were still doing me, they had any idea of who I was. I mean, maybe some. But most were just going through the pathetic old routine because I had become part of their identity — part of their little jokes. To be known as my "friend" was another word for homosexual. I had simply become as mundane as the rest of popular culture.

I'm not saying it's any more sad and contemptible than people who flocked so recently to see *Holiday* — you know, the musical they did about Madonna's life. God, that crea-ture lived for *so long* — it was such an awfully long time they had to wait before they could get the rights to her songs. But when at last she kicked the bucket, they could finally buy out that shyster son of hers. (What's his name — Jesus? What a businessman he turned out to be.) *Holiday* is, of course, an inspiredly boring title. And how did they manage to make all those "slap my ass" songs mainstream? The people who go to see the Madonna jukebox musical are just as contemptible as the homosexuals who bought my records and came to worship me. It's about identity, selling brands and belonging; so sad, so lonely, so solipsistic and resting like an atom bomb at the hollow centre of capitalism, where commodities define us.

My father, on the other hand, was another kind of homosexual. He didn't live to buy my records. He didn't want to belong; he never even tried. The problem wasn't what many thought it was. My father didn't molest boys; he just looked like he did. And it wasn't even effeminacy, though there was a little bit of that. He couldn't help being out and open — even though there was no "out" then. So what this meant was subtle: he was too enthused about everything (but mainly show business) and dressed too well. He wore wristwatches and undershirts before they were fashionable for heterosexual men. But, most blatantly, he loved all kinds of beauty, was obsessed with it.

As you know, it is Christmas, and tonight I caught sight of a particularly tedious broadcast simply because there was nothing else to do. It featured the Georgia Boys Choir. It had a lot of black young men in it. Amazing how, culturally, we can talk about race but pretend not be talking about it at all. Anyway, the choirmaster, who was of course white, was extolling the virtue of his own pedagogy. In this case, that meant reminding the audience that he was teaching virtue by helping young men to appreciate beauty (as opposed to violence). I'm sure no one out there watching was fooled; it's no accident that those professions that involve working with youth have a natural attraction for pederasts.

My father was no pederast, but the way the audience must have perceived that fawning choirmaster in those viral

Christmas images, explaining how he was teaching young men the importance of beauty — their shining faces and mostly unchanged voices singing "make the yuletide gay" — is exactly how people must have perceived my father. You can't be so open about your love of beauty and get away with it. Men are not supposed to be concerned with beauty, unless it is the beauty of a woman, and even then, as we all know, he must make sure that adoration (which should be purely sexual, not emotional) is under control. He must not love a woman too much, too passionately, or he'll lose himself.

Strange how this attitude has still not disappeared. So much else has changed. Sexualities have come and gone, bodies have become unrecognizable in their perfection. And yet the idea of masculinity and femininity is still with us. I am tempted to quote Foucault on power. But it's even more profound than that — a nostalgia, again, for differ-ence, for friction, for the "rubbing up against" in its most primitive and basic form, which is just so eternally sexy. No one knows who was born male or who was born female anymore, and no one seems to care. Gender is irrelevant. And yet our masquerades are ineluctably linked to hard and soft, dark and light, weighty and airy, sweet and cruel. There are no real men anymore, but there are so many con-vincing imitations. The transsexuals predicted we would all become indistinct in-betweens. But nobody really wants to be an in-between. (There's that word again. It is truly one of my favourite songs.)

I must admit that sometimes I still get the urge for plastic surgery. Apparently it wouldn't be too difficult to actually set my head erect upon my spine. Even though I have a special bed, like the famous Elephant Man, who died trying to lie on his back, I do so yearn sometimes to stretch out and sleep flat.

Anyway, to return to my analogy. My father was that

choirmaster, completely recognizable as a dangerous out-sider, opining piously about his love of movies, vaudeville, stars, songs, costumes and lighting. He was, remember, a natty dresser. And he was, simply, drawn to men. He liked to talk to them, wine them, dine them, amuse them — it was all he wanted from life. Of course, he was also the perfect husband for my frigid bitch of a mother. Anyway, when they finally drove him out of town, when he finally realized they wouldn't hire him anywhere, he just simply retired from life. My father died of meningitis in a shack; no one can ever understand it — it's all so perplexing. I mean, I was still so young. I was a child and he did not communicate with me . . . formally. But we were close. And I knew what he was doing. It was a Manichean struggle; it was the flesh and the spirit. He had decided he couldn't be a father to us if he couldn't be who he wanted to be (i.e., a man who loved men). And if he couldn't achieve self-respect being who he was, then it was best for him to disappear from our world.

I have proof of his struggle in the form a letter he sent my mother. I found it in the garbage. It is still crumpled, but I had it framed. It says, in quite lovely, elegant hand-writing: "I haven't drunk anything for some time now and don't intend to as long as I keep away from it." That he would seek pity from my mother — a woman incapable of *any* human emotion, especially pity — says something about his judgement. So does the pathetic idea that by "keeping away from it" he could cure himself. And I'm sure this wasn't just about booze. It was about his body, about the body in general, about its tyranny.

I visited him, and saw where he lived, and looked into his eyes. My mother didn't want me to do any of this. But I made Virginia take me. I insisted. I could see there was a Buddhist sort of struggle going on — a veiled calm behind his eyes, and the veil was tears. I'm not extolling him because he wasn't one of the young men in a front row reaching out to me. I'm not praising him for suffering. But his devotion to me (and I know he was devoted to me even though he lived far away at the end) was a devotion that was purely his own, purely independent, purely original. He loved me despite my mother, despite who he was and despite a world telling him he couldn't love me and still remain himself. His adoration was not part and parcel of trying to be accepted by a group; in fact, it was quite the opposite. When I sang: "Zing went the strings . . ." on the radio the night he died, I was singing to one man only: to him.

I didn't mean to get onto this "father and the radio show" business, even though I warned you about it earlier. I thought you might interpret it the wrong way, and you may still. But that's one of the things I have been thinking about lately. Of course, I realize that I am an addict, and I don't have any delusions about *not* being one — or of graduating from that condition. But I am thinking about the way I divide things so carefully now, in such a controlling way: a time for this and a time for that. I dare not speak or write about certain things, or do them, because it will connect me with you-know-what. And of course I cannot, must not, go back *there*.

I think instead there is a point when a person can't live with, and doesn't need, boundaries. Dangerous talk, you will say. I am not abandoning the self-evident truth that I am an addict. For in a world in which there are so few truths, strangely, addiction is empirical. Even that antique deconstructionist Derrida acknowledged empirical truths, of opening a door or touching a table or being struck in the face and feeling the sting. Well, the tangible reality here is my addiction. But what I am frustrated with is the relentless order of my life — which I have imposed upon myself to protect me from ever straying. The loss of those minute satisfactions — I hardly ever eat old-fashioned unpackaged food, hardly ever have a sip of coffee, and I feel so guilty, so very guilty, for the occasional, very occasional, cigarette. Perhaps these activities might not, in the future, be spaced out so religiously (or should I say Jesuitically?). Is that possible? Because this tedious discipline has become my way of life. And I really don't think I have anything to fear by making tiny alterations.

I love you and never want to leave you, but part of love is recognizing growth and change in the one you love. I think I am changing; I want you to know about it. If I were on the desperate slide to addiction, would I be telling you about all this, asking for advice? What I am saying is that I don't think it makes sense for me to stay away from homosexuality, or homosexuals. This fear is based on a false notion, which I have already explained — that they killed me, or that I cannot control my feelings about them, or I do not understand what happened to me when I was so close with them. It's very clear what happened to me, and I have no desire to go back to where I was. Being obsessed with Dash King is not a signal through the flames, it's not a signal of any kind, nor a hint, or a bad sign. It's simply an interest — that's all.

Here is Dash's next paper (dated approximately one month after the last). The monthly missives emailed to his advisor were partly an academic duty — the pressure was on for Dash to write his thesis. And if he were to procrastinate, there was always the danger he would drift into the vast, uncharted desert populated by those who never finished their theses. (This happened, eventually, as he died relatively young, before he could finish.) So it was important for him to make contact with his advisor in order to not jeopardize his funding.

As we can see from these papers, several things were happening — not the least of which was that his scholarly writing was quickly disintegrating into personal memoir. At this point he wasn't completely cognizant of the process. It seems he felt that confiding in his advisor was somehow relevant, though obviously digressive. The material below is ostensibly about the Shakespearean authorship again, as King is speaking of his disappointment with his lack of success at organizing a conference. But it quickly meanders into confession.

Let me give you a little more background. I know the details of his personal life because I have communicated with a professor who was a student at the University of Toronto during Dash's declining years at the turn of the century. He was an excessively beautiful and cheerful man who caught Dash's eye. Now he is quite old — but still very cheerful — and seems to remember quite a bit about what Dash was up to. Apparently Dash had organized a small meeting of University of Toronto professors in an attempt to interest them in the idea of a Shakespeare conference. The conference was to centre on the subject of Shakespeare and sexuality, which was of course an acceptable area of inquiry at the time — in the context of the New Historicism (which quickly became old) of Orgel and Greenblatt. New Historicism purported to juxtapose literature against history, without insisting that history should necessarily be thought of as authoring literature. At any rate, there were all sorts of ways in which such a conference might have been justifiable and fundable.

What's interesting about Dash's focus at this time is that his interest in the notion of Edward de Vere as Shakespeare had clearly superseded his interest in Shakespeare's sexuality. My talks with the cheerful academic who knew Dash (his name is Trevor) have been revealing. He and Dash were drinking companions. Trevor was friends with many attractive young male university students, as he was a graduate student when he first met Dash, and later an assistant in the "Department of Difference."

It's interesting that these departments were named (even when they first came into being) in a manner that predicted the erasure of sexuality as a subject of study. They were such sad things — these departments of "Difference" and "Equality" (there was even one in Brussels dedicated to "The Othered and the Abject"). Of course, since sexuality as an academic pursuit would soon be on the wane, it's almost as if the university administration realized it was best to name these departments in a way that might also suit any other emerging academic issue — disability, transsexuality and indeed the transhuman being the issues that eventually ate — or I should say devoured — departments that were originally devoted to race and/or sexuality.

At any rate, Trevor and Dash were drinking buddies, and Trevor is a veritable treasure trove of trivial yet indispensable personal information about King. Trevor informed me that Dash — until he tried to organize the Shakespeare conference that quickly became a turning point in his life (the failure of the conference was a huge blow to him, as you will see) — had been trying to control his addictions. After the conference failed, he began falling prey to his most pernicious habits. Trevor claims Dash was addicted to poppers. (This could explain his eventual heart failure.) Dash associated poppers with late-night promiscuity and alcohol. He was also prone to paranoia, unable to smoke marijuana and was, according to Trevor, afraid of chemical drugs of any kind. Dash had, for many years, controlled his obsessive attendance at the gay bathhouse by limiting his visits to the early part of the evening, and imbibing afterwards, thus avoiding the dreaded poppers.

I don't know how familiar you are with gay bathhouses. Of course, they haven't existed since the paranoia about disease grew to such epic proportions. (Strange, isn't it, how unconcerned we are with consequences of our actions, and yet the fear of disease is omnipresent.) The gay steambaths had little to do with steam, or even baths. If you want to learn more about them, there are some cyberbaths that apparently provide a lot of fun for those nostalgic for the experience. These sites are a fair — though obviously mediated — representation of what the real experience was like. People today would find the actual experience alien and discomfiting — for there was much real, physical, sexual contact. (Although the contact was under controlled conditions. Condoms and lube were made available, along with suitable sanitary facilities, etc.) This is, of course, completely alien to present-day sexuality, which rarely involves human contact at all, at least, that is, above ground — or commonly.

In Dash's day, sex was still linked with propagation, even though people feared that homosexuality might wipe out the human race. It's quaint that people might have thought that, isn't it? What actually happened was that matters of convenience, issues of population control and the fear of disease made it more practical for human beings to be conceived in test tubes. In fact, at the turn of the last century it was, paradoxically, people who called themselves heterosexuals who campaigned for a safe, sterile method of procreation that did not involve intercourse.

The steambath was a series of tiny rooms that one could barely move around in — rooms the size of closets. This was certainly ironic. Gay men fought so long to get out of the closet, only to find themselves cruising the darkened hallways and tiny rooms that were so very much like closets in search of a passionate embrace. The tiny sex rooms also resembled prison cells. Indeed, the prison motif was played up in establishments (as it is today in cyberbathhouses) — barbed wire over the doorways, sexy little prison windows, that kind of thing.

So this was where Dash would spend the early part of his evenings, followed by drinks with Trevor and the students at the university. It was a sad and lonely life — at least, in terms of the sexual practices of the time. For there were other "gay" people who were not only still having actual sex with each other, but falling in love, getting married, experiencing romance. Dash got drunk almost every night — remember, for him this was controlled, "good" behaviour because he separated his drinking from his cruising. When Trevor asked Dash why he enjoyed this lifestyle so much, he said, "I'm not very good at sex." This certainly smelled of paradox for someone who had sex so frequently. So Trevor suggested, "Does that mean you're practicing?" which apparently Dash laughed at, or rather Trevor couldn't really remember what his response was. At another point, after the death of his Shakespeare conference, Dash was very depressed. He confided to Trevor, "I don't really want to go to the baths, but I have to because my boyfriend won't have sex with me." Trevor became instantly sympathetic — he's a very sympathetic type of fellow — and wanted to talk to Dash about his "problem." But Dash became defensive, saying, "It's not because my boyfriend and I don't have sex." He then specified, "That is, we don't have sex, but it's not because of that." Trevor, who had a notion of himself as a kind of amateur psychoanalyst, tried to probe into Dash's promiscuous habits and reluctant boyfriend, but had little success.

It was also during these discussions that Dash revealed that his interest in Shakespeare's sexuality had turned primarily into a fascination with the authorship question. Trevor was confused by the switch, and again the conversation was a drunken one. But one night at the bar, Dash apparently frightened some young wet-behind-the-ears undergraduates from the Department of Difference by banging on the table and yelling, "It's de Vere. I know it's de Vere! I can't stand the lies anymore! I have to expose the lies."

Once Trevor had calmed down the undergrads and had found a private corner on the patio, he was able to get Dash to explain that "the lie about a heterosexual Shakespeare is actually less appalling than the lie about Shakespeare himself." On further probing Dash said, "De Vere was definitely a fag, but what drives me crazy is the way the academic establishment refuses to discuss him...." Or something to that effect.

Trevor's revelations concerning his drunken talks with Dash shed a glaring light on Dash's disappointment in the writing addressed to his advisor. It's obvious that Dash's depression over the conference may have been the cause of his disillusionment with academia, and may be related to his tragic romantic life. Here is the passage:

> Antonio:
>
> I want to relate something that is really upsetting. You may think that I am blowing it out of proportion but I want you to know that I am not. At least, it's important to me, very important, and something we really must talk about. Or you simply have to listen. Here, let me write this to you. I'm sorry I'm not being very articulate. But I'm deeply, deeply angry. I'm going to tell you the whole story. It all has to do with organizing the conference. I might as well tell you right off the bat that I'm not going to try to organize a Shakespeare conference. I've given up. As far as I'm concerned there's no point; all my enthusiasm has gone. The first thing I want to say is that I apologize. I feel terrible for

getting everyone together and asking for advice and then copping out. I wouldn't be pulling out if I wasn't so discouraged and upset. As you know, in my spare time I have been reading a lot about the authorship question. You've been very kind about it, as you are always kind about things — and you haven't seemed particularly disturbed about my pursuit of these ideas. I'm new to academia, as you know, and I thought that even though the ideas I am interested in are considered radical by some, controversy might be important to a conference.

Well, I'm beginning to understand that specialization is all-important, and that your acquiescence on this topic may have to do with the fact that you are not a Shakespeare scholar, or even an English professor, but a prof in gender studies. I find it shocking that people can be so sensitive about their areas. What if I suddenly decided to have a conference about the idea that identity politics was dead? I'm not sure you would go for it — not because you are not a nice person, but because it would just be too controversial for your area. Maybe I'm wrong, and maybe I've picked the wrong analogy. I'll just get on with it. Anyway, my interest in Shakespeare authorship has been my secret agenda in terms of this conference. I know I first suggested that the subject of the conference might be Shakespeare and sexuality, which everyone, including Dr. Braithwaite, seemed to think was a good idea. But of course I wasn't being completely honest, especially with Dr. Braithwaite. Of course I'm interested in Shakespeare and sexuality, but I'm also quite interested in the authorship question. And I was hoping — more than hoping — planning — that the conference might have been devoted not just to Shakespeare and sexuality, but could feature a few panels on authorship. Specifically, I was hoping to invite Dr. Mittenstatt from the University of Massachusetts who is the first American scholar to write a thesis on the notion of de Vere as Shakespeare. (Just Dr. Mittenstatt, just him, just one scholar on this topic, among — how many — thirty or forty?) Well, anyway, as you know it's been very important for me to get Dr. Braithwaite's approval and support and I was really looking forward to having lunch with him. Neither of us was going to be at the university last Wednesday so he invited me to his house for lunch. I was very flattered by this and this probably adds to the general humiliation. You know how difficult it has been for me to make the adjustment to academia from the world of the theatre. I've never really felt accepted by the literary community because I'm an out, gay writer. (You've been very encouraging to me on this subject; it's not because of you that I'm insecure. In fact, the opposite.) As you know, Dr. Braithwaite's wife, Amanda, is a professor here and also a prominent poet. I'd never met her, but I've always kind of admired her, even if only because of the way she tosses her hair around at meetings of the graduate department. I mean, they make quite a handsome couple, don't they? He is elderly but still very, very muscled, well-built, blond-bearded, distinguished and such a kind man — and kind to me — while Amanda looks like a dominatrix, or at least a woman in charge. I'm kind of afraid of her, but in a worshipful way. So when Dr. Braithwaite said, "Why don't you stop by and have lunch with us," I thought I might be having lunch with the scholar and his wife, the prominent Canadian poet. I really was looking forward to it, which makes the whole thing super-humiliating. I wish I could abandon this need to be "accepted." It's the bane of my existence. You'd think that, being such a rebel in my writings, I would be able to handle being an outsider on the Canadian literary scene. Well, I can. But what I can't seem to handle is being abandoned at lunch.

I met Dr. Braithwaite at the Broadview subway, and he was going to drive me to their home overlooking the public swimming pool. But as soon as I got in the car, Dr. Braithwaite said, "I'm sorry, something has come up and we won't be having lunch at our home." Here is where it gets a little sketchy. I'm sure it's possible that something did come up, and that this was not an excuse. But you know how people use that phrase "something has come up" — it's almost always a textbook euphemism for "I've decided I don't want to spend time with you." Now, I don't think this would have been coming from Dr. Braithwaite himself, who is a very nice man and is always very cordial to me. I can't help thinking of Amanda. . . . I could just hear her saying, "Oh, I'm in a mood today and I have to finish that sonnet and I just can't bear having lunch with Canada's pre-eminent gay playwright — not today, could you just put him off?" I know that's what happened; I'm sure that's what happened. And you know, it doesn't matter if it is a preposterous idea, and it is. But the fact is that I will never be accepted by the Canadian literary establishment. And I would like to pretend I don't care, but I do.

Anyway, the whole thing set my paranoia off, but I vowed to myself that I would be a good boy and have a nice lunch with Dr. Braithwaite because I had a Shakespeare conference to set up. We wound up in a coffee shop because it was all that was open in the neighbourhood. "Will this be all right?" he asked. He is so nice — I just couldn't say no. Well, we sat down and everything was very warm and chatty, and we really got to know each other. Did you know that Dr. Braithwaite is starting to lose sensation in his fingers? He must be sixty-five years old if he's a day, and it made me very sad to think about it. He was trying to be blasé, and he is the very epitome of the absent-minded professor. But all I could think of was, does his dominatrix writer wife with the perpetually flippy hair, does she know about this? Is she taking him to clinics, or is she just too busy writing the next great Canadian poetry collection? So I was feeling very sorry for him, and he was giving me lots of great advice about the conference, trying to work in some Dekker stuff because that is also his area, you know, which I expected and was completely open to. Then when everything seemed perfect, and he said he was going to contact people he knew, like Stephen Orgel (I was very impressed!), I thought the conference was in the bag. So we were finishing our coffees and I decided to just throw in a little question about Shakespearean authorship. I didn't anticipate his response, not for one moment, and even though it was quick and casual, it hit me like a ton of bricks.

"So, I was hoping," I said in an offhand way, "that I might invite maybe one scholar who could talk a little bit about the authorship question." "Like who?" he asked. And I didn't think there was anything wrong yet. "Well, like Peter Mittenstatt," I said. "And who is he?" he asked politely. "Well, he wrote the first PhD thesis on the notion that Edward de Vere was Shakespeare," I ventured. "Oh —" there was a pause; it was endless; a pause I will never, honestly, never, forget — "well, you couldn't do that." He said it just like that, just like it was the most absurd idea anyone had ever had. "Why not?" I asked. "Because," he said, still looking very sweet and grandfatherly, "if you did that no one would come to the conference." "Literally?" I asked. "No," he said, "I'm afraid they wouldn't."

After that I tried to make conversation and be polite and smile, but I knew it was all over for me. I mean, so much is over. Why would I want to organize a conference when the whole reason for me running the conference — my major interest, the Shakespearean authorship question — would not and could not be a subject for discussion? I felt betrayed. Not by Dr. Braithwaite, who I still think is a kind man operating in a cruel and stupid system. Yes, I have to say it's cruel. And I feel completely betrayed by it. And I don't want to have anything more to do with it. What I don't understand is, if it's so ridiculous to think that de Vere is Shakespeare, then why would it matter if one stupid and irrelevant academic were invited to attend the conference and argue in favour of the bungheaded theory? Why, instead, would that make everyone boycott the conference? What are they all afraid of? And how could a man as kind and brilliant as Dr. Braithwaite treat me as if I had just farted in public when I brought up the subject? Is the emperor wearing *any* clothes?

Okay, I'll stop. It's becoming clear to me that there is no place for me in this world. I was driven out of my theatre company. Why? For being too gay, for championing gay, when gay is clearly over. At least, in the way I knew it. And now the only academic subject I want to talk about is verboten, and I am condemned to silence. I feel that when it comes to me, the rest is silence, because what else do I have to say, and what is the point of talking?

You don't have to answer. But maybe you will understand why I have been late with my latest draft.

Thanks for everything,

Dash

The *Hamlet* reference is melodramatic but appropriate. Shortly after this, Dash abandoned not only his thesis, but any effort at constructive living. I don't expect you to like Dash; he is eminently unlikeable, self-obsessed and self-destructive. And I'm not saying I like him, just that I am fascinated by him. Is this just nostalgia? At my age, I think I can be forgiven a little nostalgia. But I don't think that's really what it is. Dash's self-destructiveness is rooted in a direct relationship with a discernable reality; that is, he knows he can destroy himself. (It is so difficult to destroy yourself these days!) But also, his obsession with Shakespeare is not only rooted in a time and place where identity mattered, but where truth mattered. When history seemed like something that could be proved. It is romantic, and I am romantic. And though I don't want to stop talking, it is late. We have been talking practically all night — it's so easy now that I am integral. But I suppose this isn't talking, technically, as you haven't had a chance to respond. Yet I haven't needed a cigarette because I have become drunk on you. You can't imagine what a job it is to haul this carcass — and that is literally what it has become — into bed. But that's what I am going to do. Sometimes I think the only thing that keeps me alive is believing you'll listen to me. When we meet again — I am certain it will happen someday — will you buy me dresses? Yes, I would look ridiculous. It would be like putting the Blob in an evening gown, mud glittering with diamonds. But I should like that. And I would especially like you to go on again about how you cannot wear dresses, that you don't know how to wear them. But I can.

I can no longer twirl. I can no longer dance. Perhaps that's why I am playing with words — because they remind me of what it was like to dance for you.

Though I expect severity, there is something else in your tone. It's impossible for me to imitate, and I wouldn't want to. There is a coldness. It suggests I am already dead. It seems only fair to wait to treat me as dead when I am actually dead, and otherwise treat me with the common respect of one human being for another. Surely we are not beyond that? I have made many allowances, yes, for *you*. You are a fragile, special case, and your relationship with your father ... But we won't go there. I know I'm not supposed to mention that. I know our relationship will never be equal. I know you require acquiescence, obeisance almost, and it is that stone coldness of you I adore. It reassures me. There is so much love and so much hate in it. I used to receive enough serenity from the severity of your look that I could sleep at night. But there is something missing in the way you treat me now.

If only I could see you ... I know it's impossible. Ironic that in an age when it is so easy, you would not allow me this. We could easily see each other and chat in cyberspace, but you won't let that happen. And that is what I must accept. Again I am thinking perhaps I should come there — or will. Of course, there is the agony of flight. Can you imagine the cavity search? I don't think the security staff could handle searching *for* my cavities, never mind actually searching the cavities *themselves*. I hear them asking: Does this monstrous mess have holes?

Well, I can make myself laugh; I hope I can still make you laugh too.

There are warning signs that go beyond the severity of your tone, things I want to challenge, because I don't understand them. First, there is your use of the word *prepare*. As if I am to be prepared for something. Is this something academic, something to do with a final exam? But you and I are still bickering over the subject matter of my postdoctoral thesis — surely it's not time yet to prepare for that. Did the word just slip out accidentally? Was I not supposed to know this? Because I can't imagine what else I would be prepared for. I hope you are not keeping anything from me, because the one thing I like to imagine isn't missing from our lacerating arguments is honesty.

I'll get right to the point. If you can answer this question, then perhaps it will begin to bridge this gulf I feel forming between us. The gulf *must be* purely in my imagination. I'm pretty perplexed (or perhaps I should say not pretty at all, but I am perplexed) that you have found such tiny — one might even say hidden — ideas in my communication with you. And that you are so incredibly upset about it. I have sent you a missive with a long analysis and history of Dash King — who you barely mention, except to say that he is an immature individual.

That's a start. But then you go on to speak as if we are beyond narcissism. Certainly when the plastic surgeon is so available — for all but the most ancient, who are typically told they are beyond help (like myself) — narcissism becomes irrelevant. On the other hand, what narcissism used to be, solipsism, has certainly not disappeared. One could argue, of course, that as people live less and less in what used to be called the *real* world, they have become less concerned with how beautiful and rich they are in actuality, and in this way become less selfish by default. But surely the virtual world is selfishness personified, now that people's acquisitive romantic cyberlives have exponentially overtaken their tedious day-to-day existence? What I'm saying is, Dash just seems more immature than people today because he is concerned with his fortunes in what we used to call reality, with success and getting laid, notions we find antique because we can have whatever we want in the virtual world. The fact that people are still, in their own ways, immature does not mean that Dash is any less so. But it's important to put his neurosis in perspective.

Then there is the issue of plastic surgery. It is completely shocking to me that when I actually address issues of addiction and suggest that I might be able to loosen up my routine, you decide to rail against the notion that I might have my head righted upon the end of my spine (or what's left of it). In this last discussion, in case you have forgotten, I referred to the possibility that I might allow myself the odd cigarette, that I might not have to observe the rituals and routines that have kept my addictions in check for so many years, because I am now so set in my ways that I am not in danger of falling back under the sway of my addictions. This is a significant notion for an addict to entertain. However, you ignore these musings. I know you are cognizant of them (you miss nothing), but instead you become obsessed with my suggestion that I might get a little bit of plastic surgery. I don't understand what is *so* outrageous about that.

You do understand that my body is crumpled to the extent that the "L" shape that I used to refer is fast becoming a "C"? As my head seems to bend more and more towards my chest, it becomes not only increasingly uncomfortable but I become more and more grotesque. You make jokes about my physical body and I do too (though it takes on a slightly different implication coming from you!). But is it too much to ask, that we might attempt to halt the daunting curvature of my spine, and at least set my head right upon my shoulders?

And then there is the implication that I would not be considering plastic surgery if I was not also considering venturing out. Maybe there is another reason. Perhaps it's not just all about people seeing me, or being seen. You know well what could still happen if people look at me too closely, or stare at me. It's still possible they might somehow realize who I was. But that's not a big enough danger to warrant plastic surgery to protect me.

What I find more than odd is that in a long communiqué in which I talk about so many subjects, you get stuck on a tiny part of one sentence. And this is the sentence in which I say sex does not involve human contact at all "above ground, or commonly." You go crazy about "above ground, or commonly." I find this uncanny. In passing, I mentioned a truism, something everyone knows and understands though it's rarely talked about. The fact is there are establishments in which some of the real and dangerous sexual activities (that we know from the past) are still perpetrated. It even comes up in the most polite conversations now and then. Although discussion of these establishments has not been banned, we realize that any detailed discussion of what actually goes on must be kept to a minimum.

I don't think you're afraid of censorship — in fact, you yourself occasionally enjoy flouting the authorities. You seem to think, and I hope you are right, that those who wish to censor, who warn us of our indiscretions, cannot and will not triumph over technology. It is technology itself that will decide whether or not anything can or will be censored. At any rate, it is the fact that you picked this tiny detail out of my letter (along with the notion of plastic surgery) that I wish to confront.

In this context it might be necessary to speak a little bit about Allworth. I am not going to apologize for our relationship. I don't want to make you feel guilty — that's impossible, anyway, and it would be out of character. Whenever the smallest spark of that emotion does creep into your psyche, it fills you with a kind of rage that is frightening to behold. Suffice it to say, I am not using Allworth to make you jealous, or to threaten you. He could never be you. Remember when we found that self-help book from mid-century that went on and on about codependence? Well, sometimes I think you and I are codependent. At least, I am too dependent on you. I know you have your women, and that some of them may mean more to you than you are willing to admit — though I know you don't like me saying that. But isn't there a moment when you are whipping them, or penetrating them with those dildos that you so ritually boil, when there is just a little tear in your eye? An ounce of affection? Don't you ever, for instance, miss them? Do you never, ever favour one over another? I know you will answer "No" to all of these questions.

And just because I can't resist a little titillation, have you ever tried electric shock? I found a great little porno scene (they are so very, very accessible now that I am integrated; I just press a button on my old head and there's porn!) in which a very lovely young man was being shocked with some sort of electronic device. He was writhing quite deliciously. I think one of the things that attracted me to the image was that the man who was torturing him was hardly a man — in the sense that we used to think of a biological man. He was such a grotesque, withered thing. Now, I know that no one could be (and surely no one is) as aged and ugly as myself. But the reason the fantasy had such a profound effect on me was because I could see myself playing the part of the old man — crumbling artifact that I am. That I might be the one *doing* the torturing! It seemed so wonderful to me that the old man could have such an effect on the boy! Obviously it was not possible for the wizened old stick to actually shock the youngster with the thrill of love. Instead he had to resort to actual virtual electricity. I'm sure that I am not perceiving this cyberlovemaking correctly, and that you will tell me so. You sometimes urge me to take some photos of myself and have a little fun. You assert that there might be sexual interest, somewhere, in a lumpen heap such as myself — that I might enjoy some cybersex. Well, I certainly would have enjoyed becoming a part of the *actual* experience of shocking such a beautiful young man, along with the other, dribbling geezer. But I don't think, try as I might, that I would be able to appreciate cybersex the way I could, or perhaps should.

Maybe this is part of my problem.

I know you think it is.

Or maybe I don't have a problem. I know you think

I still think of cyberspace as "fantasy" and still talk of it as "virtual," and I know those are ancient terms. I know I should just be thinking of it as all there is, and that, in effect, it *is* all there is. But that brings me to my experience with Allworth. So you mustn't be intimidated by him in any way. I know that if you met him you would ignore him, consider him not worth considering. In fact, you may have already met him in cyberspace if you've been trolling. He's very promiscuous and quite an inveterate cruiser. He loves couples, or enjoys being an intermediary between two men who are married, attached, in love, whatever, servicing them, getting serviced. I'm not entirely clear on what he does specifically, and I don't know if I want to know.

He is — that is, his personality is — your fundamental opposite. To say he is worshipful would be an understatement. In fact, he might actually make you nauseous. Now, I want you to know that this fawning, this obsequiousness, is something akin to a disease with Allworth. It is not related only to the fact that he has figured out who I was. Of course, he does know who I was, but you sometimes overestimate the effect of all that. Yes, I am these days a medical marvel — though more and more like me are being kept alive these days. I must be one of the oldest, however, because I am a kind of literal artifact, a relic of another era. But we both know that very little of what is considered valuable is from the past. Part of this has to do with the triumph of historiography over history.

It's interesting how far ahead of his time Paul de Man actually was. And interesting, too, that there is a point at which Dash King gets obsessed with de Man, (as with Philip Larkin and, amazingly, Barbara Pym) near the very end of his papers. You do remember the de Man scandal? He was accused of being a Nazi, but at the same time he was a kind of deconstructionist, and a friend of Derrida.

Derrida had to deal with the scandal after de Man died and the truth came out. Derrida was a Jew, and this saved him from suspicions of being anti-Semitic. It's an odd assumption, that those who are *of* a group cannot hate that group. You and I both know that it was the homosexuals who killed gay. Once they finally had enough of it they said, We are assimilating!

The de Man scandal was focused on the notion that this man, who argued for the deconstruction of history and reality, a man whose arguments could have been used to challenge the Holocaust, was in fact a Nazi sympathizer. Or, at least, at one time he had worked for the Nazis. Or, at the very least, to be completely accurate, he had written anti-Semitic articles, or articles that could be construed as anti-Semitic, for a Nazi newspaper. Paul de Man committed this crime during the Nazi occupation of France, when French intellectuals were being pressured to toe the line. Sure, some bravely did not collaborate. But de Man did. And then he went on to proliferate arguments against the notion that there was any such thing as truth and history.

Self-serving? You decide.

De Man did ultimately prove to be right, whatever his wartime ethics. It makes perfect sense that we study history as fiction now, and that we look at it as romantic rhetoric — the way we might read a fantastical story. The whole idea that one should read history because there are lessons to be learned from it is a fallacy. One wonders how this idea could ever have had any credibility when history constantly repeats itself. As Alan Bennett once memorably said, history is "one bloody thing after another." Today we know what looking for lessons in history means: it's just reading our present into the past. So, instead, we now live in the present and the future — ignoring the past. These are the only places to live. This is a part of my problem when I look back at Dash King. How I proceed with King's text has a lot to do with whether I treat it as history or literature. And it's important that I treat it only as literature. History does not exist. This is something you must remind me.

I will now remind *you* of this in reference to Allworth. I am returning, at last, to this ubiquitous person. I call him ubiquitous because there have always been Allworths in my life. But to imagine that Allworth idolizes me because of who I once was — who I am no longer — is forgetting the modern world that we live in. And you do this in a manner I am too often prone to do. This is one of the reasons I am thinking of . . . Well, I will reveal it.

I, in fact, *have* ventured out to places where I might not have gone before, because it has finally come to the point that I can be invisible.

I mean, do you actually imagine that if I could be found out — that if someone were to notice the way I held a cigarette or (God forbid) remarked upon a quaver in my voice and said, "That's her!" — can you really imagine they would tackle me and try to get an autograph? Gay is over, thank God, and I am no longer an icon of a mercifully brief movement. Ah, you might say, "the voice" lives on — in recordings. I don't want to listen to the recordings. I refuse to listen. My own records at one time obsessed me, but that is in the past. No, all I can say is that if Allworth or some other pathologically depressed and historiographically arrested person were to become obsessed with me because of who I was . . . Well, it's too bizarre to contemplate. And he'd certainly deserve his fate. One couldn't be frightened of such a being.

I can't believe it's taken me more than 110 years to accept that I don't resemble a tragic in-between any longer. How long it takes for our self-conceptions to dematerialize! The fact is that I am not in-between anything. I am not on the verge of attractive, as I perpetually was — once. When I see pictures of myself, I marvel at how gorgeous I was, even when I was fat. How was it I couldn't see that then? No, I have fallen into the hole. And it is not a rabbit hole. It is a cancerous pile of mulch.

Once and for all, I am a creature from a black lagoon. It is impossible to recognize me. Even if I speak. Even if I were to sing — which, of course, I can't. And wouldn't. But more than that, unless he is lying to me, and I'm sure he is not, Allworth's adoration for me — which does seem over the top — is not just related to a curious antique affection he has for a fiction of the past. And Allworth does realize that the past was a fiction. No, his obsequiousness is related to a congenital condition.

Allworth is an apologizer. He believes he is doing everything wrong, and acquiesces at the drop of a hat. This is partially due to his upbringing. He comes from an Asian father and a Scottish mother. He does quite charming imitations of them that make me laugh out loud, which is something I do rarely, because it actually hurts. But ultimately the laughter does me a lot of good.

He imitates his father in a full Asian accent, very fawning, very apologetic, and one can see where one could learn the apologizing from that culture. (At one point there was some speculation that the world's culture would become East Asian. Many people learned Mandarin — and this seemed oddly comic to us at the time. Interesting that it's Turkish, now, that everyone is so eager to learn. I am, of course, not saying anything against the Turks — I never would. I owe my allegiance to the Modern Ottoman Empire, and this from someone who comes from an era when that phrase would have referred to the holdings of a man who had made his fortune marketing resplendent stools. And that was not sarcastic — I would never be sarcastic about our government. But we all know it doesn't really make much difference who is governing. Because, of course, ultimately, they are not. . . .) So Allworth's tendency to apologize, and to try to meet my every need, is partially related to a cultural inheritance from his father. But he is also an obsessive-compulsive. He was diagnosed in the test tube, actually. They knew he would come out that way. And his obsession takes the form of apologizing. I often wonder if he was born apologizing because he was sorry for being obsessive-compulsive! He is eternally sorry, and eternally worried that he has offended, gone too far, talked too much, been inadequate, overadequate, whatever. I might find it irritating if I didn't know it was a disease. This explains why Allworth acts the way he does. Yes, he knows who I am, and this has only the tiniest effect on him. But he is not obsessed with me. He is obsessed with his obsessions.

So, I must get on with it. But I hoped that if you knew what Allworth was like, then perhaps you wouldn't feel so horrible about the trip we took — the escape from my apartment! Of course, Allworth and I first met in the cyberplayground. But I quickly got the itch to meet him outside of cyberspace. Why? you may ask. I suppose it's an old superstition: people so often misrepresent themselves in cyberspace. So if I want to get to know a person, I'm interested in what they actually look like. Again, I know this is an antique notion (the idea of actuality). And even though after meeting him, I assume, for instance, that Allworth is an attractive young man (which he seems to be, to me), he could have been born something else. He could have the wrong chromosomes. Though I have heard they have been able to fool with that, too, so much so that it is actually impossible to test someone to discover their original biological gender.

I can't logically explain it. It doesn't make any rational sense — I can feel you bristling — but I wanted to meet Allworth in the flesh. This is mainly because I wanted him to know that I am who I am, not a fantasy creation. Of course, that makes even less sense, because why would anyone represent themselves in cyberspace the way I do? Why would anyone wish to disguise themselves as a coagulated blob with eyes, covered with a dress-like thing (it's very hard for me, as you know, to find a dress that fits). I would have to be real, only because no one has an imagination grotesque enough to make me up.

So Allworth came over for tea. And don't worry, I had cleaned the shelves of all memorabilia. I did leave up an Al Jolson album cover that I have great affection for — just because it's so antiquely "racist." (Remember racism? These days it's quaint, and if anyone is to be a victim of even the memory of it, it is us.) But I didn't expect someone as young as him to make the connection to Swanee . . . and he didn't. No, it just came out. Being with him is sometimes like being in a media interview. Of course, I am very skilled at those and used to enjoy them immensely. This is just because, as you well know, I'm best at first impressions. I'm not as good in the long haul, but I make a helluva opening night.

So, because he was asking so many questions, it seemed rude not to be just a little bit honest. "Yes, I was a singer," I said. And when he asked me how old I was, it just slipped out. When I said I was 138, he said, "You don't look a day over 134!" It was only an old joke, of course, but it was a relief to tell someone. So when he found out how extraordinarily old I am — he had never heard of anyone living past 130 — he knew there had to be some reason why extraordinary medical measures would have been used to keep me alive. I had to explain.

There is no need to worry about Allworth. He is sworn

to secrecy. And he is so incredibly frightened of me, and indeed of everyone, that you need not fret. Also, he is not the type of person to sell the information to a media outlet. I really do believe he is my friend. Frankly, I don't know what all the hysteria is about anyway. I mean, coming from you — who want so much for me to move into the future. You want me to forget the past. But you are actually accentuating the power of the past by imagining that the revelation of it would have deleterious effects. It is a fantasy of yours that the past holds a huge fascination for me. In fact, I'm through with it all. And I hated it, actually. And I am perfectly happy to live in the now. If only I understood *the now* a little better.

Anyway, the kinds of questions Allworth asks are always about feelings, illnesses and disabilities. For instance, he asks me about walking around, and why I choose the cane over a wheelchair. He doesn't ask me leading questions that would suggest he is urging me to become who I once was, or some such nonsense.

The teas have become a weekly thing. And I know at this point if you admonish me I will say something that sounds like emotional blackmail. But it isn't; it's just the truth. What am I supposed to do with myself? How am I supposed to entertain myself when you are thousands of miles away? You left me high and dry. I understand that you have a life. And that life doesn't revolve around me (though I don't doubt your love). But do you expect me to remain in Toronto and wilt on the vine? Or, at least, wilt more? I won't try to persuade you to come back, because I know you never will. I'm just saying that I'm a very old blob and I have a huge amount of time on my hands.

During one of our teas, Allworth began telling me about his sex life. It entertains me — and, of course, I don't have one of my own. He gets himself into the kinds of situations that promiscuous people so often do — because he is interested in people for sexual reasons only. Then he finds himself hanging out with excessively boring folk for one reason only: to have a look at their private parts. There isn't much he hasn't done. And his main challenge in life is getting out of the cybercompartments of those he has had sex with. Most of his social life seems to revolve around extricating himself from these sticky wickets.

Allworth found out about the place that he ultimately took me to through his work. His work, if I haven't mentioned it already, like everyone's today, involves codes. Like the rest of the world, he spends most of his time refining and recreating the digital language we all speak. One of his co-workers introduced him to a place called the Tranquility Spa — which is neither a spa, nor tranquil. The gist of the story is he took me one night and nothing happened.

The "Spa" in the name is a ruse. It is set up like an ordinary throwback to the turn-of-the-century-style aromatherapy massage parlour. You know, one of those relics of the past they allow to exist — with strict no-sex rules, of course — as museums of ancient racism and perversion, authentic even to the point of being staffed by pretty young Asian girls. There's the doorway where you pay your fare to get in, but when you go behind the curtain it's no longer government-approved. Suddenly all is dark — it reminds me of a beatnik club I once went to, even down to the odours. Believe it or not, that beatnik club was called Hernando's Hideaway — like the song! Well, this modern version, on top of everything, stunk of urine. I haven't smelled that stale smell for a long time — I think since I peed my pants, drunk and high, so many years ago.

As I say, nothing happened at the Tranquility Spa. No one recognized me. There was no mad rush to figure out who I was. One of the fascinating things about the place is that it is peopled by very strange, lost creatures. One isn't sure why they are the way they are, or even exactly *how* they actually are, because it's so dark. But what struck me was that many of the creatures had something shockingly askew. The people were not immediately monstrous — they were monsters upon second glance, so to speak. I was the most evidently monstrous person there — the one whose monstrousness was immediately discernable to the naked eye. No, a number of these people had only partial disfigurement. For instance, many were fine but for one part of their body, where the skin was no longer being held up by the bones, and you could see inside, behind cellophane or a sort of antiseptic plastic. One had the curious experience, when entering the bar (I used my cane, and you know how slowly I walk), of finding these creatures with holes in their bodies whipping themselves around — as if they didn't want you to see their somatic aporias as you inched along beside them.

These people seem to be plastic surgeries gone bad; I'm not sure what brought them all to the same bar, but like does attract like. Then, upon closer inspection, there were individuals who were held together with putty and paste. I sat beside one and was unnerved to recognize this when she turned towards the light. There was very little light except for laser beams aimed at the floor and ceiling and walls, which I noticed most of the creatures were careful to avoid. When the light hit her, she became translucent. I could see something underneath her skin; it certainly appeared to be traces of blood and bones and organs. So she was a walking — or, in this case, sitting — skeleton. And for whatever reason and by whatever method, the skeleton had been covered over with putty and paste that had become seethrough in places. I noticed she was wearing a kind of cape. Indeed, many at the bar had pragmatic head coverings.

There was certainly no indication that this character was a vampire, but it did occur to me that she might melt if exposed to the light.

There was also a lady and a gentleman who were both missing something — in one case hands, and in the other case a neck. The person whose head was sitting directly on her shoulders fascinated me. I thought perhaps it was the result of a botched transplant. The head transplantation, as you know, is an operation I long refused to have. Seeing her — and surmising that her deformity was the result of one — discouraged me from further consideration. It *was* encouraging, though, that she could turn her head, even though she had no neck. The handless man was very odd. He seemed to be making some kind of statement. After all, artificial hands are easy to come by; the technology is virtually seamless. It occurred to me that perhaps his condition was the result of plastic surgery, that he had lost the proper attachments for the nerves and musculature of hands. His arms ended quite anticlimactically. There was simply nothing there, or it seemed that way. Then I saw there were pieces of clear plastic over the end of each arm. This would have meant, of course, that you could see inside each arm. This might have proved fascinating, in its own way, though the man did not seem to want to have the ends of his arms exposed by the light.

The one who fascinated me most I call the Doll Boy. The Doll Boy was very, very tall, slender and pale. He wore loose-fitting pants and an open-collared shirt. At first I though he was translucent too. But then I realized his case was precisely the opposite. He was opaque. He was overly smooth and white — unreal, plastic like a doll, surrounded by a completely solid casing. One wondered about his history; he might have been a burn victim. He did not look real but like a mannequin. But there was also something unreal about his gestures, his general demeanour. He was long-limbed and moved with a sly grace. This suggested someone painfully conscious of taking up space — perhaps too much space. Someone who knew he was being looked at, and didn't want to be.

What struck me most about him was that he could have been — and this is completely my personal fantasy — the material embodiment of the tragic in-between. One of the logical explanations for his condition, it seemed to me, was that he was indeed a burn victim who had not reached the final stage of getting the realistic flesh glued on top. I know, in fact, that what he was walking around in was the underflesh that lies directly beneath what seems like the real flesh of someone who has had cosmetic surgery after being scalded. I know this because I once knew a burn victim who received a cut, and he didn't bleed. But his coating of fake protective underflesh was revealed. In other words, under his realistic flesh was the doll flesh — which was all that this boy had. The Doll Boy was a sad and dignified figure, at once vulnerable and distant. I couldn't help identifying. I, myself, am sad but *undignified*, and had for so many years felt unfinished — not quite there — as I came to terms with the fact that this body was all that God ever had in store for me. There would be no divine improvements, only human interventions.

Anyway, this gives you an idea of the place. The music, as you might guess, was retro. It was so old I could barely identify it. Then I recognized that they were playing a lot of freaky monster music, for instance Lady Gaga and Klaus Nomi and that Icelandic singer Björk. And Yma Sumac — do you remember her? She claimed to be a Peruvian princess, I think. But it turned out she was from . . . Brooklyn? Well, as you can see, the place suited my taste. And nothing happened. The gist of it was I was fascinated and hypnotized. And yes, I had a cigarette, but no booze. The oddness of the place was accentuated by the sale of booze. When these days all can — and do — often choose from an array of government-approved partypills if they wish to go that route, this was certainly an anomaly. But I was not interested in the booze and did not even think about it. I enjoyed a tonic without the vodka and watched the black lights make things glow like in the old days.

Indeed, my attraction for these people may have been purely because they were old, like me. If I was right and they were most of them victims of botched plastic surgery, then it is more than possible, indeed likely, that some were old (though none as old as me). Allworth seemed to have a good time observing me and giggling. I think he was pleased that I was pleased, but was also intimidated by — and perhaps jealous of — those who talked to me.

Two people chatted with me. One was the bartender, and the other an elderly woman who had unfortunate silicone injections that had slipped drastically. She appeared to have two sets of cheekbones on one side. Or was that a growth? The bartender, who was shirtless, was memorable for having a large masculine chest with no nipples. Again the questions: was he once a female who had breast-reduction surgery but whose nipples had been misplaced or forgotten? It's odd about nipples. The old adage "useless as tits on a bull" might be appropriate here. But useless or not, when we look at someone who carries all the signals of maleness — i.e., the musculature and the body hair — but is without the climactic nipple at the end of the pectoral, what are we to think? Well, useless or not, it looks very odd indeed.

The bartender was inquiring, as bartenders do, about where I had come from and where I had been hiding. I told him (lying) that I had been hanging out in cyberspace.

As I talked to him, the lady with the cantilevered face (for it certainly looked as if there were different balconies or levels jutting from it) tried to join the conversation. The bartender was dismissive of her, as if she was boring — or perhaps someone who had the habit of butting into conversations because she was in need of some undeserved sympathy. One ordinarily would think that sympathy was surely her due. But in this place certainly no one had the right to special attention, that much was clear. There could be no crying over spilt milk — the floor would have been a swimming pool of salty tears.

So that's all of it, my darling. I promise. And I know you have been waiting for a climax, a something, a tragedy — at the very least an occurrence. You have been imagining that something or someone would pull me back, or that I would be seized with an irresistible impulse. I'm sure you already have a theory that there is a suspicious subtext to what I say. In fact, I am prepared for this. I wish you luck. I know your disapproving nature — which is also very loving. You will not be satisfied unless you find something to worry about. And it is this worry that I have learned over the years to accept as love. Judgement, correction and warnings have taken the place of an embrace. I know, for instance, that if I were to mention (and I am going to) that Allworth pointed out the dark room at the rear of the Tranquility Spa, then you would undoubtedly take this as a dangerous sign. The alarm bells would ring.

Well, let them.

Allworth pointed out the backroom as a courtesy. He has a very sexual nature and it would have been rude of him to assume that simply because I am one of the very oldest creatures alive I would have had no interest in such an area. As it turns out, I don't. But I appreciated his acknowledgement that I might have such feelings somewhere still in the mottled mess of my flesh. What interested me more than anything about this backroom — which was signified by a tattered old burgundy velvet curtain that twitched tantalizingly in the slight breeze initiated by an old ceiling fan — was that at times the bizarre creatures of the bar would actually retire there. Though none did this while I was at the bar. Later I asked Allworth if he had ever been behind the curtain. He smiled in an indulgent way and said, "But of course!" I did not find this odd. Allworth still has his own youthful body, and that's good for him — as it is good for anyone — while it lasts. It would seem he's enough of a sexophile to want to explore adventures that are outside cyberspace, even with partners who are nature's rejects.

Well, now that you know the truth — for I wouldn't keep anything from you — I hope you will not blow the whole thing out of proportion. I hope, instead, you will try to understand that I want you to have all the facts, because you care. After all, our relationship is unequal. I get only tidbits of information about your sex life. And I have to drag those out of you. God knows what you are up to — and I don't admonish you for it, whatever it is.

This monologue has been quite extended and digressive. But I want you to know that I am still working on my thesis. And I am still obsessed with Dash King. So, here is some further scholarship from one of his later papers. The passage is dated immediately before his papers become completely personal (and even more fascinating and revealing). The discussion here reveals that King's scholarship could conceivably have grown into something interesting. There is no particularly rigorous argument in this excerpt, but there is the germ of an idea. By that I mean a generalizing, quite grandly around a particular, which, as you know, can be an academic advantage, but also sometimes not. Fortunately, perhaps, it is not possible to discern from this fragment what direction he might have taken with this germ for good or ill. I am interested in Dash's musings because they are relevant to my own writing. Sharing this with you is an earnest attempt to inform you and keep you up to date, but like all earnest attempts, it can certainly betray itself and become something unintended. Dash King goes on about something called the "queer feminine." I believe it is his own concept, and it might have proved interesting if only it were more thoughtfully developed:

> If I was going to write about something, I would write about euphuism. I don't see much point now in writing about anything. I am discouraged by the responses to the first drafts of my thesis. I know I'm not supposed to take any of this person-ally. I remember when I did get a bit insulted with Professor Hawkins' analysis of my first draft. He said, "This is an undergraduate response." I asked him why. He said I sounded hurt by his criticism. Well yes, I was hurt, and why can't a graduate stu-dent be hurt like anyone else? But also it really bugged me that he wanted to take everything per-sonal out of my style. This is the heart of the whole matter, as far as I am concerned. I am a big believer in the idea that style *is* content; and I think this is a very gay idea. I know it's not fashionable to talk about gay ideas anymore, especially in terms of history, because gay is not supposed to be a transhistorical thing. I guess it's not — but I think it is. But on the subject of style it just seems to me that there is a house style for academic essays and that house style is Foucault. I know we're not supposed to speak against Foucault and of course I wouldn't dare write anything against him, even

though he makes me bloody mad. Don't get me wrong, I do enjoy his writing sometimes. But don't you think it's kind of suspicious that everyone writes like him these days? Absolutely everyone? Or they write like Judith Butler. Is it just a coincidence that all academics write in the same style? Let me quote you a passage from Homi Bhabha, whose name might as well be Blahblah, as far as I'm concerned. Professor Hawkins made us read it in his course last year and I just gave up: "Levina's parenthetical perspective is also an ethical view. It effects an externality of the inward as the very enunciative position of the historical and narrative subject introducing into the heart of subjectivity a radical and anarchical reference to the other which in fact constitutes the inwardness of the subject." What? I don't get it and I don't want to get it. Words like *enunciative*, I know, are semiotic code words. I should know them — but you know what? — I can't be bothered. I can't be bothered because it's just bullshit jargon. You made the mistake of supporting me in my attempts to write in an understandable and straightforward fashion, and I am grateful for that. I thought it was great when you said to Professor Hawkins, "You're right, Dash's thesis proposal is far too readable, he must make it less so." I know I'm privileged, because I'm white and all. But I'm still a faggot — even though that doesn't seem to count as a minority status anymore.

If you look closely at most academic writing, you'll find that not only is everybody parroting Butler and Foucault, but most of them don't have anything half as interesting to say. (You can wade your way through the Foucault and Butler jargon, but at least you get a payoff now and then.) The people who are parroting Foucault and Butler are usually women and non-whites. I know that sounds sexist and racist, but all I'm saying is that these people have a lot at stake; they are outside the academic establishment and they think by appropriating this lingo they are going to get in.

All of this accent on style makes me think about Shakespeare's ultimate style play, *Love's Labour's Lost*. It's a kind of satire on the academic modes of the day. I guess you know that some people think the play is actually a parody of Lyly. I'm pretty fascinated by Lyly and I think I could write about him if anybody was willing to listen. (I know they're not.) Those who think Edward de Vere was Shakespeare also think that the young Shakespeare was John Lyly, meaning that he wrote under that name. *Euphues*, Lyly's book, is about his Italian travels, but it's also about the love of men for men, and how that love is much higher than the love of false, promiscuous women. It's all very gay in a David and Jonathan biblical way. But what's interesting about Lyly is that his style defined an era and we don't hear much about him now. Why? Because it's an effete, antique style. But if you read Shakespeare closely you can see that it has its origins in Lyly — the style is characterized by overwriting, endlessly repeated comparisons, a long list of figures of speech. It is a very busy, rhetorical, heightened, over-embellished style that became fashionable for ladies to read in the late 1500s.

Here is an example: "Love is a chameleon,

which draweth nothing into the mouth but air, and nourisheth nothing in the body but lungs. Believe me, Eumenides, desire dies in the same moment that beauty sickens, and beauty fadeth in the same instant that it flourisheth. When adversities flow, then love ebbs, but friendship standeth stiffly in storms. Time draweth wrinkles in a fair face but addeth fresh colours to a fast friend, which neither heat, nor cold, nor misery, nor place, nor destiny can alter or diminish." It's all about alliteration and exotic images, and a list of images and comparisons.

This is Shakespeare to a tee (only not as good, not as deep), which makes you think this could be a young gay Shakespeare, cavorting about Europe before he became more profound and turned this overdone, overflorid style into something that represented something. But I see it as part and parcel of what I call "the queer feminine," a sensibility that looks at the world in a feminine way; that is, overdoes it — overdescribes it, overdecorates it. It's interesting that in the nineteenth century when euphuism was briefly rediscovered, it was scorned as effeminate and associated with Swinburne and Wilde — in other words, with gay literature. Yes, style is substance, and in the case of the gay writer the style is not necessarily hiding something. It is a response to the world that is historically (and this is what I would love to prove through an analysis of Shakespeare) grounded in an almost pathological need to compare, contrast and paint pictures with words. I don't know why it's gay and I don't know what it means — but that's what it is. I can't talk about this in terms of Shakespeare, even though it makes sense to do so, because I would have to put it in jargon. (In other words, I would have to talk about style in an incomprehensible style that would make it unreadable and inaccessible.) And anyway, no one in academic circles would allow me to suggest that John Lyly was a young Shakespeare. I give up. My best is just not good enough.

I think this passage is interesting because it shows King's last gasp at creating a queer aesthetic at a time when all things gay were on the wane. But also it's all about style as substance. I wonder if I myself am not a queer feminine character — though I suppose I am more feminine than queer, especially these days, having forgotten where my sexual organs are. But I do find the need to go on and on sometimes. I think that is where I live, in my words. At any rate, in my words to you. I don't know where all this is leading in terms of writing about Dash. I am almost on the verge of saying, "Maybe nowhere." Maybe for me he is just a kindred spirit, and I don't know why. Need there be a why?

You, who are always so always logical, will say yes.

I've gone on endlessly. But maybe that's because I am so afraid of your reaction. I am, as always, enraptured. And the distance between us makes me feel closer to you than ever. I know that is a frightening and very romantic statement.

One more thing. One of the elements I love in the *Euphues* passage that Dash quotes is that it is based on the notion that chameleons live on air — that it is their sustenance. I don't get much from you and that makes me think I am sometimes like the Early Modern chameleon. Others live on love; I live on air. But whatever you give me, I promise to love it, as I am yours, always.

I don't know where to start. I am quite beside myself. Which calls up the image of another me sitting here. And to some degree that is the problem, I think. I have been trying very much to be a good girl and live the life that has been set out for me. But I don't know if I should do it. I'm champing at the bit. Not because I'm spoiled or selfish — something you might say. I honestly don't know how you expect me to take what you say lying down. It's completely unfair, especially for someone like me. You may say it comes from all those years at MGM, of being told that I was special. Well, there you go again, like everyone else, making assumptions about me. I don't understand why I can't be treated like everyone else. Just because I happen to be talented — or *did* happen to be talented — doesn't make me inhuman, does it? Well, I've always been treated as non-human or subhuman or super-human. I really feel I've reached the point where I have nothing to lose with you. I can't even get an image of you. What I get is words, just words. That's all that comes back.

I've had it with syntax. In one of your theorizing moments you said — referring to Wittgenstein (or maybe it was just the whole last century and language theory in general) — that you can always tell when I'm in trouble. Apparently I start using bad language, or just bad syntax. You think that's what's happening now. And you went on and on about this as we academics tend to do. You wonder which came first — the syntax or the emotional problems. Oh my, maybe the disintegrating syntax *caused* my emotional problems.

How very post-structuralist of you.

Well, it's like this. The garbage you sent me is, yes, garbage. And *I* can make threats, too, you know! What you sent is full of fucking threats. Do you know what threats *do* to me? Do you have any idea? I'll tell you what *she* did to me. You know *who* I'm talking about. I'll never forget it. Since time began, it seems I've had to read this shit about me being abandoned by my homosexual father. And then the amateur psychologists chime in — "This created a longing for an abusive relationship with a man." Whatever. I wish those armchair psychologists would just spontaneously combust in their fucking La-Z-Boys. He never abused me, emotionally or otherwise. He was a wounded bird and the world didn't understand. Does he have to be a villain just because he was a homosexual?

Listen to me. *She* was the villain. Has anyone ever done a fucking study of mothers? We get a dumb rep. And by that I mean a good one. In other words, we can never be really *bad* because we're mothers. But mothers are the worst; worse than any knifing or torture. What that fucking bitch did to me! I know you've heard this story before. But before, I always gave the nod to your suggestions that perhaps it was not true. I let you think it might be exaggeration. Well, I'm not exaggerating.

I was there. I was tired, I was worn out, I was eight years old and I was complaining about the vaudeville act. To my mother, this was heresy. I had good reason; it wasn't just that we were going to have to get up early the next day and haul our asses to some godforsaken town outside of Pasadena to do an afternoon show. It was because the last time we performed there the crowd was terrible. There was no one there — and the sad little group that finally turned up abused us. They fucking threw things at us. I mean, people don't like the act? Fine, big deal. We all don't have the same taste. But do they have to throw things?

And so my mother wakes us up with the "Upsy-daisy, girls! It's never too early to shine!" She knew I didn't want to get up that morning. She just loved torturing me with her fucking fake cheeriness, loved making me unhappy. It's as simple as that. Now, why would that be? You know, there are some women who just don't like other women. No, it's true, they don't. And these women-haters are not necessarily femmes fatale. Jesus, I'm the femmest fucking fatale there is, and I love women — especially if they're smart and have a fucking edge.

I used to love Marlene. I couldn't stand June Allyson. But the difference is so easy to see. You put the two of them together and it's evident. But, you know — one of the reasons might have been Marlene's clit. June Allyson didn't even have one; I doubt if she even had a boat, never mind the little man in it. But Marlene had a gigantic one; it was like a small dick, I swear. She showed it to me. (Noël Coward was very impressed with it, by the way. He offered to go down on her, but Marlene said it would be incest.) Marlene wanted *me* to go down on her. But then again, Marlene wanted *everyone* to go down on her. I'm really not into that. I mean, I like women, *but* . . . And she absolutely understood. I think she was just pulling my leg. She really liked to shock people. But, boy, did that broad like blow jobs. I think that's all sex was to her — just getting a good blow job. She used to tell me stories about Mammy going down on her. You know, Mammy from *Gone with the Wind* — Hattie McDaniel. They met on the set of *Blonde Venus*. The whole movie was about sex, sex, sex — and debasement. So, sure enough, Hattie starts winking at Marlene. She said that Hattie knew right from the first moment she saw her that all Marlene wanted from life was a good blow. Hattie said that some women, just from the way they wave their cunts around, might as well be wearing a sign saying, *Gimme a blow job now!*

Well, anyway, Hattie really got off on Marlene's oversized equipment. I must say, this story made me love Marlene. I didn't hate June Allyson because she was a woman. I hated her because she was boring. I didn't love Marlene because she had a big clit and was, therefore, a man. Don't go all essentialist queer theory on me. Anyway, Marlene *wasn't* a man. She was all woman and full of the business. And she was so smart and so nasty — but in a good way. She could make mincemeat of awful people as she would not say one good thing about them. She loved tearing them to shreds. She did it with that Nazi drawl of hers and made it sound like she was sending them to a concentration camp.

But there's a kind of woman — usually the pinched June Allyson kind, and the kind like my fucking mother — who congenitally hate other women. Who knows why? It's probably innate, some crazy genetic thing. I know my sister Virginia was not too fond of women either, so maybe she got it from my mother. Well, this kind of woman is always jealous, always competitive — like a man, actually — around other women. Okay, so now imagine a woman like this with three fucking daughters. What luck, eh? Well, of course she's going to torture them. I used to feel so sorry for my father because he knew she hated us; but there was nothing he could do about it. I mean, mothers back then — and even now — those manipulative hags can do no wrong. Those evil bitches, someone should rewrite the book on mothers. Mother's Day should be Hitler's Birthday, and hey, how should we celebrate *that*? Get Hitler a nice card, congratulating him on his crimes? Why is it that women don't commit as many crimes as men? But oh, they do. They torture their children — it's called parenting.

So that morning we were in some sad and sorry hamlet near Pasadena on our way to another matinee. And we had to get up early after a late-night show. But mainly I couldn't face getting hit with the tomatoes. You know, years later Sue, Virginia and I would laugh about the tomatoes.

But at the time it wasn't fun, and it wasn't funny. And I wasn't having a tantrum or anything, Jesus, I wasn't lying on the floor doing a Helen Keller. I wasn't being a fucking child star; I wasn't even a fucking child star at this time. This was completely before Hollywood. I was just the prettier, cuter sister who could actually sing. Now, I may have been crying, but it wasn't fake crying. And believe me, I know the difference.

I got up and packed my suitcase and sat on it. As I say, I was crying. And Mother was in a rush like she always was. And there was a schedule. And there was just me in the room. My sisters were already in the car waiting. It was a very sad room — the room I had slept in with Sue the night before. I remember there were two single beds, and a painting of a brook and a stream and a church. A goddamn church. And there was a lamp that didn't work on the bedside table. And, of course, a Bible inside the table, and bedspreads that had that kind of grubby feel. You know, not exactly dirty, but not exactly clean. There was only one tiny round window, and it was also dirty. And there was a rug on the floor that had some sort of biblical scene woven into it.

I'll never forget that room.

So there I was sitting on my suitcase crying. My mother comes back up to get me. I was ready to tell her I was sorry for crying, and fully expected to do my duty and go down to the car. But no, when my mother saw me she was livid. Sometimes I think my mother actually resented me *because* I was such a nice person. There are people like that, you know. They feel bad because they're not nice people, and so they hate people who are. The bad people who are just fucking bad are actually not as evil as the ones who wish they weren't. Evil people who are just evil will leave you alone. But the ones who feel bad about being evil and wish they weren't — they just love to torture nice people out of jealousy.

So she opens the door and sees me there. I swear she didn't miss a beat, she just started her act. My mother was a very good actress, really she was. She didn't get much of a chance to show it in vaudeville. But when the chips were down, man, you didn't have a chance with her. Nobody did. She could turn it on and off like a fountain at Versailles. She took one look at me and she went completely dark. It was like a cloud passing over the sun. She said, "I'm sorry to see you're crying." And I fell for it and sniffled and said, "I'm sorry too." Then it was serious shit, completely terrifying, and she knew it.

"I've been thinking about it a lot and you're a drag on the act," she said. "But audiences like me," I said, hopefully. "Sometimes they like you," she said, "but the problem is you can't take it. You can't handle it. You're no good on the road. You're just a pain. So I'm sorry to do this to you, darling. But we just can't have you in the act anymore." I didn't understand. I asked her what she was talking about. "I'm leaving you, I'm leaving you here in . . ." I remember now; the name of the town was San Gabriel. That's right, like the angel. "I'm leaving you here in San Gabriel," she said. I'll never forget those words.

I was confused. I said, "Mother, how can you leave me here? I'm your daughter!" Then — I swear it — I was seven years old, remember? Well, maybe eight, but I was a young eight, at least emotionally. And remember, my father was already living in a shack. And my life hadn't been too secure up to that time. All I really had was being onstage and singing with my sisters, and, of course, having audiences love me. So I couldn't believe *that* was being taken away. But my mother really seemed to mean it. She said, completely seriously, "No, we're going to leave you here, honey; we're going to leave you in San Gabriel."

And this is the part that sounds completely crazy now, so many years later. The idea that I would actually believe that my mother was going to leave me in that lousy one-horse town sounds crazy. But at the time I truly believed her. I said, "Mummy, how can you do that?" And she said, "Sometimes parents leave their kids. Daddy left all of us. Now I'm leaving you. That just happens sometimes. You're a pretty girl and you can sing all right. Maybe someone will adopt you. And maybe, when you work for them, you won't complain so much and you won't be so much trouble, and everything will be all right. But right now, I'm going to have to say goodbye." By then I was starting to get hysterical. She pretended to comfort me, which made it even more real: "Don't worry, honey, I'm sure you'll be okay." At this point she had closed the door and locked me in the room — those old rooming-house doors could be locked from the outside. Well, that was it. I was alone in the room. And as far as I knew, because I was eight years young, it was forever or until someone found me. Of course, I started screaming and yelling, and my mother, God love her, that righteous bitch, let this go on for at least an hour. We almost didn't make our gig. She almost made us miss our gig so she could teach me a lesson.

I remember how I used to hate it when people would praise us, and she'd say, "I never spank them, you know, I don't believe in corporal punishment." No, she didn't. She was a *good mother*. Instead of spanking us she delivered the kind of torture that makes you wish you'd never been born. I will never forget what it was like when my mother left me in that room. Therapists talk about abandonment issues, and with most people it's just abandonment *in theory*. They think their parents don't love them and might threaten to leave if they didn't measure up. But my mother invented *conditional* love. She made it perfectly clear that she wouldn't love me if I didn't measure up. And, in fact, there was no point in her loving me if I didn't sing like a trooper and turn up on time. Her standards were high. And when it came to vulnerability and weakness and all the good emotions — pity and love — well, she didn't have time for any of that shit.

So you have to understand that when you make threats like you did, it must happen: you turn into my mother. I know I'm supposed to leave that behind. But some things you can't leave behind. Jesus, it's not fair for you to play on that kind of shit when you know the story. I know I've told you before — you *know* how sensitive I am about being just left. What do you want me to do, get down on my knees? You know I can't anymore. I couldn't even give you or anyone else a blow job.

You know what triggers all this shit? The fact that you demand I come up with an organizing argument to prove to your satisfaction that my attachment to Dash and his work is not neurotic or psychotic or *whatever*. What's going on here? Aren't you my friend anymore? I swear, if I could see your face it would make all the difference.

There were two ways you used to be stern with me. One was when you were defending your boundaries. I know you have a lot of them. When you were doing that, it was serious and scary. It was all about you, and I would have to dig my heels in and obey because you were more scared than I was (even though you would never admit fear, just show the anger). Then there were the times when the littlest smile would creep onto your face, because it was not about your issues at all. Your boundaries weren't threatened; you were just trying to help me and teach me some lesson. I could tell by looking at you that you were just being stern with me because you loved me.

Okay, you aren't her, all right? But it's hard for me to remember you *aren't* my mother when I can't see your fucking face. I resent your reaction to the Dash King business — it brings up all my mother bullshit. There's something about Dash that interests me. So? Can't I flirt with ideas occasionally? Can't you have unconditional love for me and accept that without demanding every observation be a chapter of a fucking PhD thesis?

Of course, you know I can go there. I can switch over in one second, and I can be the professor, the Doctor. That's what I've spent the last twenty years of my life turning myself into. My academic record is, as you know, a great comfort to me. But sometimes I wonder if that's all there is — which is an old Peggy Lee song that I really wish I'd recorded before I died. You see, I'm not superstitious about tossing out remarks that bring up the past, because that's the whole point of being where I am today, of doing all this work, of my relationship with you. I will no longer be examined at every moment and tested. The tests are over.

Okay, okay, I hear you. You'll tell me that testing me is caring for me. That I never learned to care about myself because I wasn't properly parented. Yes, yes, it's true. I don't know how to respond when people are critical. Tests are good, and it's not about unconditional or conditional love. You are not *not* loving me by asking me to justify myself.

Okay, so here goes. I will try to answer your question. You want me to tell you why I'm obsessed with Dash.

It's not just an irrational emotion. It's not some force from the past drawing me back. Yes, there may be a theoretical basis (or perhaps I should say, paradoxically, an anti-theory theoretical basis) for my pursuance of the Dash King papers. Perhaps I've been on thin ice with you — because of the antiqueness of his obsessions and their possible relationship to my past. Also, I know you rejected all that queer stuff long ago with the rest of the world. Now we live in a post-theory — or what has been postulated as post-theory — era. And we are, in fact, moving into what might be called the post-post-theory era. I am perfectly aware of that. The truth is that my interest in Dash King can easily be related to the post-theory position. I know post-theory was justified long ago, but perhaps not in this particular way.

All right, I am willing to go there, unafraid. In fact, that should be my theme here: unafraid. I am willing to go into dangerous territories. And you are, in effect, daring me. So I will. You will probably say that what I am about to postulate has already been said. Fine, but have all the implications been explored?

The implications become clear in this next Dash text. It's about the perils of deconstruction, of theory, of constructionism, of fantasy, of fiction. . . . It seems to me that the death of homosexuality was a kind of suicide. Speaking of implications, homosexuals (and specifically intellectuals like Foucault) are implicated in this. Dash clearly has issues with Foucault. Yet I would argue that his view of the world is Foucauldian — Dash is involved with the construct of sexuality, though he would deny homosexuality is a construct. But his life and his letters prove to us, so blatantly, that it is.

Let's begin with the dangers of theory (which have been well documented). I am interested in looking at extreme skepticism. Here's one, just to pick a random example: post-structuralists once went so far as to question Galileo's theory of gravity as a truism. Science tells us there have been different concepts of gravity. We know that Aristotle, when he witnessed gravity, witnessed a stone seeking out its natural place. Galileo, on the contrary, witnessed, in the movement of the same stone, the gravitationally induced movement of a pendulum. These are two different views of reality. And traditional history, before post-structuralism, would have us think that Galileo's view was the correct view, and that Newtonian physics (based on Galileo's theories) had transcended the ancient Greek view, which was mired in superstition. But post-structuralism would have us look at the two approaches to gravity as different constructs that are equivalent in value, suggesting that each view is acceptable in its own context. Neither is more right than the other. But we can see the weakness in the post-structuralist position. What does it leave us with? A world in which everything is a construct, where there is no "there" there; where there is, in effect, no reality, only relativity. Philosophers are now certainly toying with the theory that there is "no reality," and some are going further with it. I know you have done some research in that area.

I am struggling with it. I see the perils of post-structuralism, and post theory that would deny reality. I am one of those who is — as you may have already guessed — still attracted to reality. There, I have let the cat out of the bag. I am attracted to reality. Is that the "first principle" that you wish to challenge? Well, go ahead. Or are you going to say that the reality principle is okay for some but not others? That it has dangers for people like me, people with addiction issues? We are attracted to the real world. This means, for us, doing drugs in the real world. This means living, in other words, in a fantasy world *in reality*, rather than living in cyberspace, a completely fictional world. But cyberspace would be a much safer place for us.

This brings me right back to the idea that I am some sort of special person. And I thought the idea was for me to forget how special I am (which I mainly have done). I thought I was supposed to simply function as an academic, to function within that particular reality. There is also, I think, a fallacy here. The implication that arises from the notion that I can't handle reality, or shouldn't be attracted to it, is that all reality is sordid, or sexual, or dark, or sad, or dirty. But why need it be? Why can't reality be me sitting — or attempting to — at a desk and working on theory or anti-theory? I am, for one, willing to accept that reality.

And so how does this all connect with Dash? You will see from what follows that Dash himself was the victim of a gay paradigm. That paradigm was self-destruction: suicide. As much as he resisted Foucault, it was inevitable he would be caught in this trap. What was real for Dash and so many of his ilk at the decadent "end of gay" was not sex itself or sexual choice, but some fiction of sexuality. As we know now, object choice is varied, as is gender, and this is quite accepted in the modern world.

Certainly it has been no problem for our conservative government to fund sex changes as part of our medical plans. It has been no problem for what used to be called same-sex marriages and are now just called plain old marriages. There was never any problem with this, except on the part of certain — I am not afraid to say it — fundamentalists. But as we well know, though there are definite fundamentalist elements in our government, they do not actually make the laws (thank God, and pray they never do!). But they are there, lurking. At any rate, it would be pretty hard, I think, for even fundamentalists to deny the principles of tolerance that have been written into our legal system.

Similarly, it is impossible to write away the rights of women, although the concept of woman has become pragmatically irrelevant. Biology, after all, has less and less a part to play in that concept, or in sex, sexuality or conception. But what *has* of course disappeared, and gone underground, are the aspects of sexuality that were associated with gay culture — promiscuity, drug addiction and the endless encyclopedia of weird extreme sexual practices.

We all know (and I will say it again, even though it upsets you) that these things exist. Certain very sad and perverted people are involved with these things. We know that they are not healthy. And of course health, or at least survival, for the many — for as many years as possible — has become one of the ruling principles of our existence; so much of a ruling principle that we don't have to worry about it — the government just takes care of it for us.

On that note, it amazes me that cigarettes are still for sale. It's interesting that they are technically illegal. How can something be illegal, and still be taxed? Somehow this has managed to happen with cigarettes. I know that occasionally people are arrested for smoking in public and face stiff jail time, but this is very odd considering that cigarettes are legal to buy and smoke in one's own home, as long as your home is not a business or connected to another building. But you understand issues of the law and citizenship better than I.

So what am I getting at? What Dash was "fighting" for, in his own tiny mind, were all the aspects of sexuality that were related to what he labelled gay culture — drag, promiscuity, leather fetish, weird sexual practices, alternative relationships, feminine men with male bodies . . . the fictional constructions of homosexuality. This was his hopeless cause, and made his fight pathetic and bathetic, but interesting to me in its martyred superfluity. Now, it's true that Dash, to give him his due, was right about some things. For instance, his complaints about academia and jargon were echoed by others of his time. Remember Sokal's famous hoax paper "Transgressing the Boundaries: Toward a Transformative Hermeneutics of Quantum Gravity"? It was written entirely in fake jargon and published.

But it is when Dash gets into his own area of queer theory, and into his own incredibly warped, complicated and self-defeating arguments about gay life, that his tragedy, being hanged by his own favourite construction and strangled by his dearest fantasies, becomes clear. It's also interesting, in the following passage, that Dash talks so much about AIDS, and that his lover challenged that paradigm by practising unsafe sex. But, paradoxically, his lover also fit quite neatly, by doing so, into a much larger and more dangerous construct — that of the suicidal homosexual. Unsafe sex was very dangerous at the time, in fact illegal. Today we have simply made promiscuity illegal — at least, *real* promiscuity. Promiscuity in cyberspace is, as we know, ubiquitous.

So this text, which was probably sent to his supervisor, Antonio, although it is not addressed to him specifically, is tragically prophetic — especially when viewed in the context of the rumours around Foucault (of which you are probably aware). It is significant that no one knows whether or not these rumours are true, and probably never will. They are in their own way constructs or fantasies. But, at any rate, there were people who said that Foucault, who died of AIDS, practised unsafe sex. Of course, when he died, safe sex itself was a relatively new concept. But the notion was that Foucault, who ultimately believed in a shifting vision of history and fact, was not himself convinced that there was such a thing as AIDS. How could he be convinced when he did not believe that science, history or facts themselves were anything but fictional constructs? Though it has never ever been proved that Foucault practised unsafe sex, it is nevertheless an interesting theory that slips Foucault into the suicidal paradigm that Dash inhabits so neatly. But you can see for yourself:

> I have had it with the idea of writing a thesis. There isn't any point; I don't want to go on and

can't go on. Instead I am writing you this. This belongs in the garbage or in my memoirs. Do you think anyone would be interested in the memoirs of an old fag like me who created one of the world's premier gay theatres? No, no one is interested in that now. I wouldn't even try. It would be like casting pearls before swine. I have decided that if you want me to write something for you, and not "give up" writing, then I have to go on academic strike, and by that I mean I am unable to write another essay or weave any more theories. They have nothing to do with reality. And I'm not going to play the game called "What is reality?" Anybody who comes to me with that kind of question I would class with the philosophers that Bill Cosby talks about in his comedy. The philosophers who ask, "Why is there air?" ask a question as valid as "Does reality exist?" Any dummy knows the answer to that: it doesn't matter if reality does not exist, it's all we've got. So I'm not going to even try filling this paper with anything that resembles jargon. And I'm not going to talk about Shakespeare anymore. I'm going to talk about myself. This is going to be very embarrassing for you, I'm sure. But it's much more embarrassing for me to write. But since you said, "Don't stop writing, write about anything," it's your fault. How embarrassing will this be for you? Well, you said you lived through the sixties and that that time was more embarrassing than anything — you took part in nude sit-ins, the whole bit.

Okay, so not only am I going to be personal, I am going to be as personal as possible. I am in love with an impossible person. He is an impossible boy. And he doesn't love me back. He never will. And that is why I love him. I love him more than anything and I get absolutely nothing in return. There's a novel by Barbara Pym called *No Fond Return of Love* (that is a quote from some poem). Okay, I admit it, I'm a big fan of Barbara Pym. And Philip Larkin. Yeah, Philip Larkin. There's one for you. I can't be bothered to look up the Pym quote and I'm not going to. The novel is about a woman who is in love with a man and follows him around everywhere but doesn't expect anything back. The man returns her love by falling in love with her daughter and trying to seduce the girl because he's basically a pedophile.

My boyfriend is very beautiful but very shallow. His inside doesn't match his outside. I don't know if he was ever a good person. He is very lovely, but empty; he is blond and slender and he looks like he is about fifteen years old. He is in fact twenty-three. He was born in the Yukon. There is something of the Yukon about him — he is remoteness itself. His name is Jason Swallows. That's his name; I didn't make it up. His name is a pun, because he does swallow — other men, not me. I lie about him to all my friends. I tell them that my boyfriend and I used to have sex but we don't any longer. The truth is that we never had sex. He won't let me. I don't measure up. At least he is honest, and I know where I stand. I don't care; it's the hopelessness of my love for him that keeps the relationship fresh. I will never be close to him because he won't let me, and because even if I could be close to him, there would be nothing for me to be close to. He embarrasses me in *all* social situations. I just can't be with him in public. People stare at him, and me, they can't believe we're together — but we aren't, not really. And they can't believe that I'm madly in love with him, or that we have anything in common. Well, we don't. What do I get out of the relationship? I'm free to pursue other sexual relationships. He doesn't interfere with that, because he doesn't care enough about me to care. What does he get out of our relationship? He gets the privilege of hanging out with someone who is a very prestigious member of the gay community. He likes that. I would say he was a star fucker if he were actually fucking me.

I'll tell you what we do in bed. (You wanted me to write something, anything, so that's what I'm doing.) I like to lie beside him and kiss his pale white shoulder. And then I jerk off. I jerk off while I'm looking at his body. Occasionally he lets me run my hands over it. Then he lets me cum. I make a little puddle on his thigh. And he just lies there. Dead, for all intents and purposes. But mainly he's just bored. I don't mind. You know what else we do? Sometimes when I'm in the bathtub and he has to come in to take a leak, he pees on me. He pees on me, and I drink it. This can't be healthy. Why? Because my boyfriend is HIV positive. We will never have sex, ever; there is no chance of it, because of this. He is perfectly unattainable. He will also probably not be alive for much longer. His health is good now, but it won't be long, until . . . You see, he likes to practise unsafe sex. I like to try and practise safe sex on my nightly escapades, but these days, especially, when life is pretty bleak, I find my only solace is a nice stiff drink or two and some poppers and a young body that will remind me of Jason. Jason Swallows. Other guys — not me. That's probably how he got AIDS. After all, he likes to take it up the bum from gigantic body-builders who are much more *adequate* than I am.

So that's my life. Do you think I can work that into a thesis? Or perhaps I should turn it into art. The only problem is that nobody wants to read anything I write anymore. I'm not telling you this so you can save me. I don't want to be saved. I remember when I was young I didn't want to be a homosexual, and the reason was because I had a vision in my head of an ugly old man sitting beside a table in an empty apartment staring at a single light bulb, wanting to commit suicide. I never wanted to become that man. But somehow I have become him. Thanks for listening.

The letter is unaddressed and unsigned and the bar-renness of it is devastating. One wonders what it would have been like to know this unpleasant individual. I expect he was, at this point, the type of person who truly lived only in his alcohol-induced, nitrate-driven sexual fanta-sies. It's interesting to me also that he does not mention Shakespeare. Yet this is certainly his most Shakespearean moment. The letter is like a Petrarchan sonnet, though the style is mundane. Dash wants nothing from his lover, nothing in return. This stretches the medieval notion of courtly love beyond its wildest dreams — until it becomes the Elizabethan ideal of courtly abuse. One sees echoes of Blanche DuBois in his description of himself; the lonely man sitting in an empty room is Blanche's "ever since then there has only been this one candle." It is more than masochism; in the context of homosexual ethos, this is the death of a culture that is suicidally obsessed with the worship of youth and beauty. So much so that Dash can do nothing but lie in bed beside beauty and kiss its shoulder. Finally, he allows himself to make an embarrassed, sad puddle on beauty's thigh.

Dash has wholeheartedly bought into the tragic paradigm of homosexuality. It is his fate. Whether he has chosen it or not is a deeper philosophical question. I would say he is certainly trapped in it. I think that after the death of homosexuality, its most noxious obsessions were usurped by mass culture. Certainly what the Christian fundamentalists saw as the dangers of homosexuality did, in fact, become a part of our cyberworld. Nothing that is "old" or "ugly" has any place in our culture now, except of course in the musty groves of academe. Here, monsters like me are kept alive by those few who imagine we might be valuable artifacts. But even that is being questioned. You have told me that some have questioned your work with me — that the grant you received to encourage me, and to examine me, has been challenged. This is despite the fact that you were careful to place the work in a modern context, and certain to make it evident that it was not a "historical" project.

I have no proof for the assertion that when homosexuality died our culture effectively ate the values of that culture. For instance, I have no proof that the homosexual obsession with youth and beauty had any influence on us. Indeed, what was so important when those we used to call "the terrorists" won was whether or not tolerance was still to be a cultural value. Would the government brook no quarter for homosexual culture? Looking back, which I know is dangerous, I wonder if what saved people like us, and various kinds of human difference in general, was when the cyberworld became sacrosanct — when web activists decreed that it was exploitative and unfair to police the web. At this point, the powers that be realized it was simply impossible to control cyberspace. Cyberlife was to be unquestioningly protected. Now anything is permitted on the web; nothing is permitted in reality. Everything is allowed as long as it is not real.

I'm sure this has relevance to your concerns about my visit to the Tranquility Spa. Let me put it this way: there is no death penalty anymore. And what would death be to me, anyway? Aren't I too old to murder? When the prospect of my demise hangs over my head daily like the sword of Damocles, the worst that will happen to me is that I will be incarcerated indefinitely for my crimes. I have not committed any crime *yet*. But I speak facetiously. I will not commit any in the future. And anyway, I can't imagine the government locking me up; I am a cultural artifact. At the very least, my body will undoubtedly be carefully saved and ransacked by cyberbiogeneticists after my death. More than that, my present existence is already a kind of incarceration. It is so difficult for me to walk, and my monstrosity certainly makes the possibility of human contact a grim and unlikely prospect.

But for once I didn't mean to digress. I want you to be aware that I don't think my little bar visit is the melodramatic issue you have made it out to be. That's why I want you to understand the scholarly value of Dash King's papers. Please don't worry any further about some return to my previous addictions.

So let's return specifically to Dash and the issue of the death of homosexuality. What's clear to us now is that AIDS not only killed homosexuals, it killed homosexuality. We are none the worse for it; no one misses it. Dash was prematurely grieving its death, eulogizing it with a kind of negative capability.

If one examines the male love poetry that was connected with Virgil and the pastoral poets, one observes a melancholy that morphed into A. E. Housman and his elegies for soldier boys. It's not only twentieth-century gay literature that is suicidal, countless plays — from *The Children's Hour* and *The Green Bay Tree*, to *The Boys in the Band* — all featured tortured, self-flagellating, suicidal queers. This tradition is transhistorical in Western culture. In fact, it is my suspicion that if Dash is right, and Shakespeare was de Vere, and was trying to escape his own doomed pederasty, he may have avoided, in his sonnets, the direct homosexual address of one of his contemporaries, as it may have become inflected with an already clichéd pathetic flavour.

Little is known about Barnfield, a much-forgotten poetic contemporary of Shakespeare's. To imagine, as Foucault does, that there was no homosexuality in Early Modern culture is naive. Barnfield, in his blatantly and clearly homosexual poetry, talks not only of sodomy (Foucault's favourite concept) but of love and affection and even possible partnering between men. But the tone is invariably sad, melodramatic and tragic. So there is reason to imagine that Shakespeare was all too wary of the pitfalls of a homosexual aesthetic. Whether he was de Vere or not, Shakespeare may have been writing about a homosexual love affair (or more likely a pederastic one) in the sonnets, but he is deliberately cagey about it. This is not because it was forbidden. Barnfield's odes can attest to that. (He does apologize for the homosexual content of his poems in an introduction to one of his books of poetry, but this hardly indicates that he was persecuted, or that his work was banned for being homosexual.) Perhaps it was merely that Shakespeare didn't want to write bad, melodramatic, bathetic poems that — like Barnfield's — were drowning in pastoral excess and melancholy. He didn't want to write bad Elizabethan homosexual pastorals.

These issues were rarely dealt with in discussions of the master poet. And now that Shakespeare has become irrelevant, these issues may never be dealt with again. But though his work may be unsalvageable, ancient and written in what is essentially a foreign language even to those who speak English, the sexual politics of Shakespeare's period *are* fascinating. The epitaph for Shakespeare's sonnets was written by Northrop Frye when he said, and I am paraphrasing here, "If we took the sonnets literally, we would have to believe that Shakespeare was in love with a stupid teenager, which is simply impossible." Impossible indeed. Truth is impossible — always has been, always will be. Perhaps you and I can at least agree on that.

At any rate, this is the vast tragic homosexual aesthetic legacy, and when AIDS appeared, we saw a depressing march of AIDS plays and novels from the homosexual community — not depressing because of their subject matter, but because they were so badly written. As Susan Sontag rightly observed, AIDS did for the theatre exactly what tuberculosis did for it — and by that I mean absolutely nothing. I am convinced that the dance of death that people sometimes spoke of as having followed AIDS was not the return of promiscuity. (Although this happened in the early part of the last century, before sex became almost universally — as they used to call it — virtual.)

But the birth of gay marriage — the kindly gay priest swathed in rainbow colours — this was normalcy; the dance of death for gay identity. For gay was, and always had been, tragic. Gay was Blanche DuBois, *Death in Venice*, the coughing, sputtering Greta Garbo in *Camille*. Those who lived, married and somehow managed to produce a successive generation were no longer gay. Certain post-AIDS fags quite hopelessly clung to the tragic paradigm. Dash King is perhaps not the most brilliant, but is certainly the most characteristic, example of a generation of men who, though there was undoubtedly a medical cause for their disease (which has now become only as serious as diabetes), were also seduced by a suicidal paradigm that AIDS fit right into. I am not the first to theorize this; I have found an obscure essay by Casper G. Schmidt, a psychoanalyst from South Africa who died of AIDS in the 1980s. He theorized that AIDS was a kind of mass hysteria, a suicidal complex shared by gay men as a result of their treatment at the hands of the religious right. In *The Stonewall Experiment*, Ian Young proposes that gay men have believed their own negative publicity to such an extent that they marched to their own death.

This is not to say that AIDS didn't exist. But one notices that the construction begins not to be associated with homosexuals after the turn of the century. This is because homosexuality was at this point dead as a cultural force. AIDS had become, along with the cancer battle, anti-terrorism and environmentalism, a global issue. This means it became a family issue — focused on hope and the future, as all issues are these days. We know now, of course, what happened to environmentalism. One wonders not so much at the stupidity of mankind but at its naïveté and self-centredness. It was sentimental to imagine that we could save the world or that our human lives were, in fact, the centre of it; instead we had to settle for science and cybernetics, which has allowed us to live on a dying planet in unreal bodies that, increasingly, do not require air to survive.

And then, unfortunately, the so-called terrorists won. (Well, I know they were not really terrorists, but they were Arabs, and dressing like terrorists, so they might as well have been.) But that may not ultimately have been such a bad thing. No one could have run the world without some compromise. I am trying to fit my analysis of Dash into a larger worldview. You have deemed it essential that I prove I am obsessing over him because I have something of scholarly import to say, not because I am neurotically and perhaps dangerously attached to his story. Well, here goes. . . .

Dash's life proves both Wilde and Foucault correct, while at the same time establishing an emblematic example of the failure of postmodernism and post-structuralist theory: our constructs eat us. What is the next step once we are aware of this perilous fact? Are there to be no more constructs? Or must we simply acknowledge those constructs? But how do we do that when they are so hypnotizing? This is what post-post-theory must deal with. But the fact that I have finally, through Dash King, arrived at the threshold of post-post-theory is, I hope, for you, promising. I will even go so far as to say that your concern over my actions actually warms my heart — what's left of it — despite my fear of abandonment. When I finally banish the panic, I can see your affection for what it is.

I'm going to float another boat here, one I sincerely hope you won't find upsetting. I would like to suggest that I have a, perhaps, inappropriate attraction for what I wish to call *the real*. I think you would agree. Or maybe you would say that I have not fully adjusted to the cyberworld. This is my problem and a problem for anyone who loves reality: the real is being phased out. The reason most lives are essentially lived in cyberspace now is partially because living in *the real* is nearly impossible. No one wants to be there. It is inhospitable, whereas cyberspace is the land of pleasure. My inability to immerse myself in cyberspace has always been an issue for you. Why, especially in this advanced stage of decrepitude, shouldn't I take advantage of the life I can create for myself sitting in my chair (or doing as close an imitation of sitting as possible)?

Of course I should, and it is for this reason that I

am, paradoxically, considering making a final visit to the Tranquility Spa. I can hear a strangled cry coming from you; I know you will find this upsetting, and it might even lead to more threats. (My darling, I know you don't and can't mean them.) Let me be clear. The desire to go back there one final time is to prove the kind of power the place *doesn't* have over me. In other words, I want to go back to prove that it doesn't matter whether or not I go back. I want to make a practice of my resistance to the past and all its toxicity.

I did not mention something that happened just as I was about to leave the Tranquility Spa. I left it out because I did not want to upset you, and yet I fully expected to tell you. I am thinking now that, after taking in my analysis of Dash King, solid proof for your cast-iron brain of my commitment to analysis, not emotion, you will just drop the notion that I am flirting with the past. Know instead that I have arrived at a new level — one in which old temptations mean nothing to me. How am I to be a scholar if I can't cultivate the distance between self and reality that is *de rigueur*? It is only by putting myself in the very centre of a ring of fire — by risking a scalding — that I can move forward and change my life.

It's been nearly one hundred years! Think about that; it's been nearly one hundred years since I was a drug addict. I am a different person. And it's time for me (and for you) to stop fearing the past. As if I will suddenly implode — or explode — from my exposure to the heat. We know that the real is of less and less importance. I use the phrase *the real* instead of *reality* because it can be argued that because so many people now live in cyberspace it might, arguably, be what is now reality. After all, many no longer leave their houses, for many reasons — the dangers of temptation, difficulty breathing, even superstition. The fact is, what used to be called cities have become withered husks dotted with hypocritical museums like my Tranquility Spa.

So why would I leave my house, especially when it proves so difficult for me to ambulate? Precisely *because* there is still a shadow over my life — a lingering, lurking, pestilent fog reminding me that I may "regress" again. I won't. You may say drug addicts cannot "visit" drugs. I am not suggesting that. I never would. But it is very important for me to confront bravely the ambience, the breeding ground, of so much past trouble. Those sights, sounds, smells and, more importantly, ideas are still, for me, associated with the past. To know them is to resist them — with the full confidence that such resistance is possible. When I have resisted, and know I can resist, I will be more empowered, to use an antique term, and be able to, as Wordsworth (alarmingly, I am quoting *him*) said, find "strength in what remains behind."

So this is what I did not tell you. As Allworth and I were about to leave the Tranquility Spa, I heard a remark that perhaps was — or perhaps was not — delivered in my direction. It came from the woman with the cantilevered face. Whether or not it was said to me, or not just to me, and not just in my direction — and whether or not, in fact, I heard correctly what was actually said — is a substantive issue. But then again, not really. For even if I have imagined the implications of what this creature uttered (for she is definitely a creature — not of appearance, but of personality), then the power that such an imagining potentially has over me is still important to confront.

The woman with the cantilevered face looks, as I mentioned, like a monster. There are things sticking out of her skin — though they're still under — that should not be. And those projections are not bone. They are something else: plastic, spit, putty — perhaps tumours. Who knows?

Of course, some tumours cannot be surgically removed. I am fully aware of that. It is more dangerous to attack them than to leave them be. I presume she had had her eye on one of the other male creatures at the bar (or those resembling males). I presume this from her remark. I think it was aimed at the handless fellow. At any rate, it was he who left just before her remark. And I thought (though I may have imagined it) that she had been looking at him out of the corner of her eye. This is an odd and funny expression in her case, because her eye really did have a corner. There was a gigantic, almost pointed, bump that jutted out of her face just atop her eye at the end of her heavily made-up brow.

Upon his listless, desultory exit, she, who was sitting in close proximity to me, turned to the bartender and said, with a committed conspiratorial glance, "There goes the man that got away."

I guarantee I would not have remarked on this, indeed would have let it pass, if she hadn't also glanced at me. Why? Here is the conundrum. Of course she could have done so simply because I was in her line of vision. But this is contradicted by the fact that her line of vision, in terms of myself, was obstructed by the protrusion above her eye. To look at me, she had to make a specific effort. This she definitely did.

But the meaning of the remark may depend on her age. Certainly it was impossible to be sure of how old anyone in that bar might have been. Though none are ever as old as I. If she was young, let's say under one hundred, then it is unlikely she would be making reference to me or that song, at least not consciously. But if she was over one hundred, then it is completely possible that she knew to what and to whom she was referring.

But, another hurdle: even if her remark was a reference to the song, was she aware that the person who once sang it so famously was sitting next to her, disguised as a malformed lump of flesh in a dress? It is highly unlikely. Reflecting on circumstance like this might seem, at first thought, to be unfortunate or even, frankly, desperate. I know what you are going to say. Did I go to the Tranquility Spa expecting or indeed yearning for such a moment? Is it my fondest dream to be remembered? Is that world of fame — where I once lived and dreamed and carried on so brightly — a part of me that I pine for? And has the loss of that world made me half the woman I once was? I am certainly half of what I once was physically, barely even a woman. In fact, the quantity of real flesh and guts still attached to me is probably less than half of what there once was.

This is perhaps the most important thing for you to understand. But it's difficult for you, for anyone, to comprehend. Fame is now so very *over*. Everyone is famous, and no one is famous. Everyone is an author and an expert, and so nobody is. The cyberworld makes us each at once invisible and renowned, each celebrated in our own way, though often anonymously. So I can understand how you and many others might be ignorant of the machinations of what used to be called fame.

In the distant past I made pronouncements about my duty to my fans. I think I may even have said, "My fans are my life" or "I live only for my fans." I'm not saying that these remarks were nonsense. It's simply that their meaning has been misconstrued in a romantic, not pragmatic, manner. What should be remembered most of all is that I was a worker — perhaps not in the strictest Marxist sense. After all, Marx had a famous disdain for performers and artists, calling them effete. Nonetheless, I am a practical person. I was brought up that way by my horrific mother and by the famous absence of my father. From the first moment they pushed me onstage until my last appearance at the Palace,

I was singing for my supper. And if some saw in my performances an urgency, a life-and-death quality, there was a reason. I was literally hungry. Of course, I am not denying that there was artistry in my work. Far from it. I crafted all of my phrasing and pitched the meaning (or just threw stuff away) with enormous precision, sometimes even subconscious precision. But even the crafted pain was part of the act.

This is where it gets complicated. When you are a performer like I was, the act is not an act. It is real for the time you are doing it. You *are* living it. You are there, onstage, you are not somewhere else. You do not "phone it in," as we used to say. But how can I make you understand that my all-encompassing, nearly Buddhist live presence was not fulfilling any need inside myself for love? I often think how sexist this notion is! How often do they say, still, that Frank Sinatra was enormously talented? Quite often. (He was also literally enormous, according to Ava Gardner.) But do they ever suggest he was singing because he was lonely, or simply desperate for love, or affection, from the masses watching him? I'm not questioning Frank's honesty as a performer. I certainly don't question the sheer virtuosity of his delivery. God knows how he found it or sustained it. But no one ever suggests that his artistry was a pathetic plea for attention. Yet they do this — *have always done this* — to me.

Of course, one might theorize that something transpires psychologically inside a performer after she has appeared onstage night after night, managing to be fully present. The performer begins living her life onstage as much as off. The two states become, in a sense, interchangeable. But does not the surgeon who is fully present at the operating table live in his work as much as I lived in mine? And if he was working nearly twenty-four hours a day, as many do, would he not begin to confuse his art — surgery — with his life?

For what I did, ultimately, was work. *It was a job*. People forget that because I was so good at it that I made them forget. And by calling it work, I do not wish to demean it. I can think of nothing more fulfilling for my life or any life than to be consumed with productive work (my puritan undergarments are showing).

If I were to miss anything about being a star, it would be the work itself. That is why toiling as a scholar is so fulfilling, because it is merely another kind of work I may throw myself into or against, sometimes successfully and sometimes not. When, in interviews — and remember, publicity was part of my job, after all — I went on about my love for my fans, I was still working. I wasn't lying. I loved those fans and needed them, because they put food on the table. One can't understand this if one wasn't brought up in vaudeville. The cheque from the hands of the theatre manager re-materialized as food. When my mother left me, the fear of abandonment was real, but it wasn't only emotional abandonment that frightened me. My mother had been responsible enough a harridan to drill into me that at any moment we might all starve. My true fear of being cut out of the act that day in the hotel room wasn't just a fear of being alone, but that I might end up dead on the street. Such lessons never leave you, especially during a depression — even if you end up at MGM.

So, am I going to try to convince you — with all of this talk about craft and work and practical considerations — that fame meant nothing to me? I will not. But it meant far less to me than you might imagine. At a certain point I realized that if I could reduce fame's importance in my life I would develop a real personal life. During the fifties, when I struggled with my weight, it was actually a struggle with this very thing. After Vincente and Sid, I came to the understanding that both of these men were married to the "star" as much as they were married to me. There was nothing wrong with them. They were both fine fellows in their own ways. But they certainly were fellows, in my eyes, and still are. And is that the way you talk about a man you love — or did love once?

Vincente was so very much like my father in all the shamefaced debauchery that took place — though most of it was in his imagination. I knew (how could I not?) what was going on — I'm not that dumb. If you look closely at his movies, you will notice something about the male extras. They are all beautiful — like the hothouse-flower ushers that curled their tendrils around my father. In fact, that is the way one can differentiate the work of a homosexual film director from a heterosexual one: examine, closely, the walk-ons. You will notice that in a heterosexual director's work the male walk-ons are undistinguished, hardly noticeable. But the little typist, or the girl who is passed on the street on a cold snowy night? These figures are of a radiant beauty, striking, earth-shattering, dumbfounding, nearly alarming. In a homosexual director's oeuvre, the tiny parts played by typically young men are populated by distinctly unforgettable youths. In Vincente's case, they were lithe and also dark — very like the ones so favoured by my father.

This didn't upset me. I was so wrapped up in my work that I had little time to be concerned about love. Although I did think I was in love with Vincente then. I think I was unconsciously drawn to him. And this is what they all say, but it happens in this case to be actually true. The closeness I desired from my father, but didn't achieve, was certainly a factor. But this was not, as some have suggested, because Vincente was a father figure. Quite the opposite was true: I had enormous pity for him. I noticed his pain, his anguish and his shamed faces immediately. His desperation to prove himself by giving me Liza touched me so much that

I would have done anything to make him happy. After all, I was making Vincente happy, not so much by pleasing him, but by loving him in spite of it all. Vincente knew I knew, and I knew he knew I knew.

Sid, on the other hand, was the end of the line, romance-wise. I sensed I needed something, and the easiest way to get what I needed was through my work. Ergo, I married my manager. Thank God he was a helluva manager. I kind of missed the fact that he wasn't shamefaced and vulner-able. However, those were two of the many things missing. But after Sid I realized I was over being attracted to men who wanted to manage my career. Mark was definitely the last straw when it comes to husbands who were in love with the *star*.

With Mickey, at last, I found someone who was responding to *me*. Although it's important to remember that if you were famous the way I was, when fame meant something (I sound very old now because I am), you could not eradicate that element completely from relationships. On one level my identity — because I spent so much time onstage — *was* my work, my famous persona. So they would only love a part of me if a partner were to ignore that aspect. But there were still people at that time I knew — June Allyson was one of them — who didn't believe that Mickey was in love with the "real" me. Or perhaps she hated him because he *was* in love with that? Nobody ever wants you to change, even if staying the same means decaying and dying. "But he's a kid," June said. "A sweet kid, but still a kid."

Fuck, this infuriated me. I would like to know why the fuck June Allyson thought she should have a say in it. I mean, she can say anything she wants. But do you know who that woman married? I mean, she wasn't above Joan Crawford–like choices. What was going on with Dick Powell's barber — the one who physically abused her? (Or so she claimed.) How screwed up is it to marry your ex-husband's barber? I'm sorry to be so judgemental, but she really has never been charitable to me.

Okay, fine, she was a notch above Crawford, who for years fucked anything that could walk, male or female, as long as they could further her career. I wouldn't have put it past her to fuck a goat if it had studio connections. And then, finally, paradoxically, she got all pious and married the Coca-Cola salesman. Of all the hypocrites in the world, the pious are the most sickening. And what a thing to get pious about. "I'm marrying a big thief businessman who stole lots of money by addicting children to fattening sugar drinks that gave them diabetes." Let me tell you, no one was happier than me when the powers that be made soft drinks illegal. Who would know that Muslims would be so obsessed with soft drinks? More power to them. It just tickled my funny bone back in the day to think about Joan Crawford bedecked in jewels and furs and giving press conferences about her marriage to that fat old thing with glasses. Nothing against fatness — it would have been fine if she was actually into fat. Many people *are* into ugliness, thank Christ. But no, she just realized she was too fucking old to get any hot tail, so she prostituted herself to the corporation. Congratulations, Joan, I'm so glad you fully realized, so late in your short life, that all along you were really just in love with money.

If I sound bitter it's because I am. June Allyson and the rest of the assholes came down on me about Mickey and that pissed me off. I don't think June Allyson actually had sex — I mean, an orgasm. What's worse is that she wouldn't want one. And she wouldn't think it was *right.* Dick Powell, who she was married to most of her life, was a bit of a numbnut with no chin. Although you know what they say about men with no chins — God giveth and he taketh away.... Sinatra was a chinless wonder. June knew exactly what was going on with Mickey. In that one crazy period with her husband's barber when she was always drunk she was probably deep down somewhere chasing sex. But she couldn't allow herself to admit it because she was such a prude.

And everybody else knew what was going on with me too. This old lady was getting laid *and* getting appreciated. I'd finally found somebody I got along with. And I was just being *myself* for a change. And not just onstage. I finally realized there was a difference between art and life. But, of course, I get punished for it because he wasn't a boring, fat, ugly executive with spectacles and money. Mickey was fucking hot, and he was *nice* to me, and it was *me* he was with, not *you-know-fucking-who*.

I'm telling you all this because of the comment made by the woman with the cantilevered face. It would really piss me off if it were to launch you on a lecture about fame and its dangers. Not that I miss it. Sure I got a little kick, a tiny jolt from it. You know, like when a baby kicks? But the way Lorna kicked, not the way Liza kicked. Liza was one crazy baby in the womb. I actually believe she started rehearsing for our big appearance at the Palace in *there*. Very disconcerting at the time. . . .

Yeah, when Cantilevered Lady looked right at me, there was a frisson of old pleasure. But that's just about pride in the work, that's not fame. Fame is pernicious and evil. If anybody tries to tell you differently, they've never experienced it, never been there. If they had been, they would know how hard it is to be famous and still be alive. So, once and for all, I did not do it all for the fame or my fans. I did not love them. I did not need them, dream about them. But, on the other hand, living as a recluse, pulling a fucking Garbo and getting all hysterical when someone notices the gravel in my voice or the way I smoke a cigarette, is that sensible? Isn't it just a waste of time? Not only is fame over, but *my* fame is long over — and I am pleased to be rid of it.

I hope and dearly pray this discussion has done something to change your mind. It's been overly long and involved and digressive, but I miss you so much. Sometimes I could just taste you. I hope I will be forgiven, for I am flawed. I am returning to a very old excuse, but one that is tried and true — perhaps not with you and not now. I am human, and I am not perfect. I know you are human *and* perfect (as you never cease reminding me). At the same time, you are much less of a cyborg than I am. I respect that. You were born a human machine though. And I know those pretty little femme girls that you enjoy whipping now and then — do, now and then, in the words of Cole Porter (who said it all), *get under your skin.*

I miss you and I am not lying. Can I be clearer? To the best of my knowledge I am not lying. But as Derrida says, lying can only be conscious or else we are merely misspeaking. "Have I misspoken?" she said, I think, ungrammatically.

Thank you for listening. I promise I won't be a bad girl, and that's all that matters — along with youth, and the future, and tolerance, and cyber-reality, technological progress and the continuous free flow of information. Am I — perhaps in this singular, coincidental instance — correct?

N ow I'm going to get down to it. I can't help it. You've upset me too much — as you know only you can. That's the problem with love. And this is why I wish I had never discovered it in the first place — and did, with Mickey, no matter what you or anyone else says. Love makes you vulnerable, and that's supposed to be a good thing. But is it? Because then you're easily hurt and when you're hurt you hit back. So that's what it's going to be. But remember, I'm doing this only because I love you.

At one point in the middle of your vile response — vile, because there is so very little there that is not accusation — you stopped to briefly mention how much you love me. I remember how we used to fight back in the day, before you moved away. I remember how your eyes would flash with hatred as you lashed out. It was because I didn't live up to your expectations. It was because I wasn't intimate enough. Because I hadn't yet learned how to bring down my guard and be close. Do you remember how you yelled at me?

I'm going to get very psychoanalytical here.

Why are you so wounded?

The amazing thing about my life is that no one ever molested me. The closest I ever came to that was from my mother. I do think, in her case, an argument can be made for emotional molestation. I'm not diminishing the effects of physical or sexual abuse; I'm certain they are in many cases lethal. But equally lethal is a mother who consistently violates your personal boundaries by manipulating you and tricking you into being vulnerable and then pulling out the rug. At every moment she knew what she was doing. She knew how to hurt me and she twisted the knife. Did something like that happen to you? Because you get so ... angry. I know you will hate me asking, but I don't care. I really don't give a fuck anymore, and why should I?

The things that you said. How am I to remind myself — even when you do so yourself — that they are being said out of love? Your tone is too close to my mother's. Maybe it's time for you to think about Cynthia. Yes, I know about Cynthia. How could I not? I know she is the reason you moved away. I'm sure you don't want to talk about her, and

I'm only going to say one thing: don't tell me *you* never loved. Don't tell me *our* friendship has been the only close relationship you have ever had. I know you loved Cynthia, and that she cut your heart out and ate it for breakfast. And I know the reason you won't come back here and see me is because of *her*. You are afraid to set foot in this town because this is the town where your hurt is. These are the streets you walked with her, the street corners where you kissed. And if I know you as well as I think I know you . . . the alleys where you fucked her.

And now, to get really psychoanalytical, is it possible that whatever abuse you suffered relates to your attraction to sadomasochism? I know that I'm supposed to give that aspect of your life a philosophical pass, on the basis of some wretched Foucauldian notion of power that you have wrenched from post-structuralism — just to suit your purpose — after rejecting the rest of it as old-fashioned. Maybe it's not about power. Maybe it's just about someone who hit you. And now that's all you can associate with love.

This is an old opinion, I know. You may observe that I'm pulling out my old bag of tricks to wound you. Do you see what you've made me do? Madly thrashing about, I'm like a child. I'm like Helen Keller on the floor again. No, I'm like Patty Duke, *herself the actress*, trying to discover what acting actually might be — ineptly clawing the air with what was supposed to be impotent rage, beside a trash can in a badly lit pseudo-alleyway in *Valley of the Dolls*. They claim they had to fire me because of my famous instability on the set. But let me tell you, it was all about Patty Duke. I could *not* be around her. Oh, she was nice enough — but can anyone say deluded? Whoever gave that listless little thing the notion she could act? The fact is, anyone could have played Helen Keller — all you had to do was grunt and groan. And besides, no one else could imagine what it would be like to be born deaf, dumb and blind and still be alive. So Patty Duke could get away with anything. And she got an Oscar for that little Houdini act.

So are you hurt now? I hope so, because I'm letting the fangs out and turning into my mother. Why shouldn't I?

Let's start with this accusation — because this is the lowest and vilest of them all. You suggest that I am drinking. First of all, no, I'm not. And I resent the accusation *so much*. I also resent the fact that I should have to report to you. I know you have acted as my counsellor and my support over all these years, but you are now

a) not here

and

b) not my jailer.

Your physical absence, and your inability to act as witness to — I don't know what else to call it but my growth and change (I know these days I actually physically resemble a growth . . . oh the irony!) — is problematic.

The proof you look for is "in the pudding," as you colloquially jibe. You say that when I get bitchy and angry, and swear it's proof that I am sitting in a drunken solitary stupor. I find this ludicrous. Yes, it's true that my tone wanders, and is at times excoriating in the extreme. But I didn't know I was to be subject to the style police.

I have addressed the subject of style over substance and its relationship to homosexuality. In this context I don't think anyone has really addressed the relationship between Oscar Wilde's aestheticism and post-structuralism. I don't see that there is any difference. Foucault, in fact, suggests, at the crux of his defence of his particular brand of historicism, that one should look at historical traces — evidence, forms, rules and so forth — *as reality*, rather than trying to find *the truth* behind them. Foucault's project could be viewed from a purely aestheticist angle. In other words, for

Foucault, the world is a work of art (or its systems are, at any rate). This view of the world is not unrelated to the Renaissance view that saw the world as a book that had to be deciphered, interpreted, for fundamental truths.

Of course, Foucault does not believe in any such truths, but the methodology, the hermeneutics, is similar. One must look to the form — this is Adorno as well — to find the content. So I would say your obsession with the style of my text is a kind of old-fashioned and somewhat hoary post-structuralist aestheticism. I will not hesitate to disagree with your position. In my case, the form is most definitively *not* the content. In other words, a suddenly brash tendency to curse my mother, or to rail on about Munchkins, is not proof positive that I have lost my noodles or that I'm sitting with a Manhattan in one hand and a smoke in another, poised to pop a Valium. More accurately, I would probably be curled up with a drink, not sitting. Isn't it interesting that as we age some of us become more fetal? My perpetually curled-up status makes me less and less like a very old woman and more like a baby. But, speaking of Valium, can one even get it anymore? I doubt it. . . . The drugs I was addicted to are so old. How could I even manage to *be* a drug addict these days?

What I think you are finding hard to digest is the fact that I am changing. And this is only natural, since you have not seen my advanced deformed condition, which is literally making history as we speak. No one has lived so long while morphing into something beyond detritus — almost becoming afflatus. I imagine that eventually I will become a noxious gas. But will I still think? One thing is sure, I'll still be angry at you even if I'm merely vapour. At the age of 138 (at parties I'll admit to 135), I am still alive and vital. More importantly, I am still learning about life, who I am and who I might be.

What, after all — since I'm feeling profound, and not the least bit drunk — is death? It is certainly something I must approach soon. After all, I am not immortal. Or let's put it this way, even if I could be immortal, I would rather not. I know there is the theoretical possibility of immortality today. There are those who are picked for the experiment, those who are supposedly lucky enough to experience it. But that's not for me. And that certainly isn't because I enjoy the disintegration of my body or its poetic disfigurement, because I desire the inevitable decay. Instead it's because there needs to be a terminus. That is part of what makes us human — along with compassion, wit, vulnerability and the *ability to make mistakes*. I stress this last because you seem to value it so little.

When I first came to Toronto, so many years ago — after my first and nearly effective liver transplant — there was a place near the bus station with a very interesting name. (I arrived by bus; it was thought that the bus station was the least likely place anyone would look for me.) It was called the Terminus Baths. I have no doubt that it was an inglorious destination, and that many a depressed homosexual had died on his knees in the hot tub there. But seeing the name was one of those moments when I embraced my own mortality — which at the time seemed imminent. It was the glorious humanity of the name. This was before AIDS, but when the kind of suicidal ethos that permeates Dash's letters was in full swing.

One remembers the disbelief in Lady Bracknell's question. She distrusts someone whose "point of origin is a terminus." But it was Wilde's fellow Irishman Beckett who so aptly reminded us that we give birth astride a grave. I am not looking forward to dying. But on the other hand, after living such a long life, some of it as what was once called a "star," I will look forward to death as concrete confirmation of my humanity. I deserve that, at least — as everyone does — but I deserve it especially, because in my audacity I imagined I might be able to evade it. I don't mean through anti-aging technology, but by imagining my recorded voice would outlive me. It will, but those recordings are nothing but what we used to call *the real*. Anyway, I don't wish to think about immortality. It is anathema to me, the way death is to so many others. One need not be reminded of the persistence of the desire for immortality; all fundamentalist religions are based on it, as is the religion of our present government.

I remember when I was recuperating from my second liver transplant, I had to go to Hamilton, Ontario, for tests. It was a repulsive but strangely attractive town near the larger city. They had an effective cancer treatment centre. I dutifully took the same bus every day to Hamilton, which usually travelled a well-worn route — the local highway. One day I was travelling back late at night after an evening appointment at the hospital, and fell asleep.

This was during the last century, when I was very concerned with being recognized. I resembled an emaciated version of my former self (which was at times also emaciated). I had worn a man's hat — shades of "Get Happy." But I wasn't thinking about these kinds of things at the time. I had slid down on my seat, and the hat had dropped over my face. So there was none of *that* kind of danger. But when I woke up, the bus had gone off course. It wasn't charting its usual path, and had left the highway behind. We were riding through unfamiliar territory. There appeared to be a mountain on the right, with what looked like grim little shacks perched in the valley on the left. Some of the shacks had sad but inviting chimneys pumping out the toxins. It was winter. I remember passing by a church that offered

"Salvation" with an aggressive sign. There was a muffler-shop sign offering bargains with a similar abrasive tone.

I woke up to these unfamiliar and not particularly heart-warming images in a haze. It seemed to me we were lost. Had I taken the wrong bus? And for one terrifying moment it occurred to me that this was death's bus, a vehicle leading us all to the *terminus*. I was being driven to my death. I even for a moment imagined that we had slipped into an Einsteinish universe. I was on a bus without time, one that had veered off the edge of the space-time continuum.

It turned out that the highway was closed and the driver had simply decided to use a back road. But this was a reminder of the fear that those who embrace God must feel. They fear that death is a vast unknown, a chasm suddenly opening beneath their feet. It offers unknown untold horrors, unless, of course, they embrace God. Then there is the vision of heaven in Gounod's *Faust*, where God sits on a giant throne like the Ghost of Christmas Present, surrounded by costumed dancers and a table laden with food. Well, for me death is neither a vast chasm nor a hearty dinner. It is just the terminus. And it will make me at least more human than I perhaps have ever been before.

But to get back to the matter at hand . . . What is it with these digressions? I am not drunk. I am, I will admit, still so in love with you that even when I hate you as I do now, I miss you terribly. So there we have it — the eternal, inscrutable puzzle. But to get back on track (and perhaps prove that my digressions merely characterize me, though they are not character flaws) — I am not drunk. So hopefully that issue is settled: I do not drink or take drugs. One cigarette now and then is enough for me. And I seem to be able to control that (but not the expense of it). You need to understand this because there are changes happening in my life that I want you to understand because I do love you. But this may prove easier said than done.

Now, specifically, to your other points . . . You move to an intense and equally paranoid analysis of my remarks about the woman with the cantilevered face. You seem to find it significant that I thought you would be upset about the fame issue. You imagine you are one step ahead of me, and very perceptive about my faults. The key, you say, is not that I resisted the lure of being recognized — you seem to think there is very little danger of this now.

Perhaps you are right — how long it takes us to part with the image of our young selves! I have a mirror placed upon the floor, because I am too short to stand up and look at myself in a normally positioned mirror. Looking at myself from beneath is more horrific, and thus startlingly real, in just the right way. I will not give up on myself. I want to be a witness to my disintegration. This is not to save myself, but to be as fully conscious as I can be until the very end. It's comic to me that even though I remind myself on the quotidian of the monster that I have become, the image of the wistful *in-between* is still lodged in my brain.

Anyway, you correct my assertion, saying you don't suspect I am hypnotized by the prospect of re-experiencing some of my past acclaim. Perhaps I have convinced you with my argument that it was only ever the work that mattered. Sometimes I think, however, that you enjoy belittling my theories. Condescension is part of your strategy. I will, I'm sure you believe, come to distrust my own judgements of myself.

Anyway, you quickly and arrogantly sail into analysis of my discussion of June Allyson and Mickey. You assert that I go on about June because there might have been some truth in *her* condescension towards Mickey. This would just be silly if it was not so appalling. June Allyson never had insight into anything: I thought I had made that clear. At the heart of your argument is the *coup de grâce*. That I wish to talk about my love for Mickey alarms you. You also find it ridiculous. Without criticizing Mickey, you suggest that it was a period when I was not myself because of the drugs. This kind of statement indicates an ignorance about taking drugs. I know that you desire so *much* control over your own life that you refuse to self-medicate in any fashion.

But remember. I was with you on that strangely endearing night when you drank nearly a fifth of vodka — *very quickly*. And much to your chagrin and mine, you tried on one of my dresses. Of course, nothing I owned would ever have fit you. (How am I to know now if that still holds true, as I have no image of you today to compare with what you or I once were?) Well, first there was the self-consciousness of your drunkenness. It was a metadrunkenness, a postmodern inebriation. You kept repeating, "I am drunk, I am drunk, look how drunk I am. I'm going crazy, I'm losing my mind. I'm going to do crazy things!" And then you insisted on raiding my closet. "Wow! I am going to try on a dress!" you said. Then you ran up to my room, threw open the closet and chose the most glittering garment with the most dramatic décolletage. When you yanked it on, I thought you might rip it. Praise God for spandex — you didn't. Then you stood in front of the mirrors in my room and pranced around saying, "I'm going to give it a try, wearing a dress. I really want your opinion, how do I look, should I go out to the transgender bar in this?" And then because you were metadrunk you insisted I seriously answer your question.

Obviously you looked more than ridiculous; you had pulled the dress over your own jeans and T-shirt and were making no effort at all to be feminine — although you did model it in a very pointedly clumsy way. I'm pretty sure you pulled on a pair of my high heels. This just exaggerated the ridiculousness of the enterprise. There wasn't much effort on your part, and that was the point. And what was so funny was that finally you made a concerted, sincere attempt to be a femme. You vowed to me, over and over again, that if this adventure with the skirt didn't work out, then it would be your one and only foray into girlishness. Eventually you staggered up to the attic guest room where you were staying, still wearing my dress, threatening to slap on some makeup and depart for a night on the town. You didn't. In fact, many hours later, after I had gone to bed, you woke me up to hand me the dress. "I tried," you said. "I tried to be feminine, I really did. It just didn't work. The dress didn't look good on me, did it?" This little bit of self-fulfilling prophecy was meant to be comic, and it was.

But this bizarre incident was the one and only time I know of when you attempted — in this rather puerile manner — to lose control. It just served to put quotation marks around the whole notion of you being inebriated or experimenting with drugs. This means you have little or no understanding of what I went through so many years ago, or what drugs meant to me, or anyone else. There is only one sense in which this might be a good background for addiction counselling. It's true, for instance, that you could not possibly enable me, when you have no idea even of the pleasure one might enjoy during a voluntarily induced drug experience. But your lack of relevant experience means there is a serious gap in your understanding of my situation.

This, as I understand it, is your analysis. Here, also, is my prediction. You think that I am talking about Mickey far too much. You think that I am romanticizing my relationship to such a degree that I have forgotten the reality, or have just wilfully abandoned it. You begin talking about this by saying, "Whatever Mickey's merits are . . ." This, as I understand it, is supposed to represent the epitome of generousness. It is your attempt to see things from my point of view.

But there are several problems with your approach. First, despite your cleverly disguised denials, you are ultimately dismissing Mickey. You see him at best — and these are your very words — as "an ineffectual person." Mickey was not ineffectual. He wanted to be an actor and I think he could have been. But then there are some people who are not capable of achieving anything themselves; they are simply better at facilitating brilliance in others. Mickey was very good at this with me. He was an amazing support and a witty and charming companion. He was also, significantly, not afraid to love. It wasn't being taken from him — as it seems to be with so many — instead he gave it freely. It was as if it was his mission in life to do so. I have never met such a kind, loving person.

You say that if I were truly "in love" with Mickey, then I would have kept in touch with him. But you know that this was impossible, that I was in and out of the hospital and on the verge of death for nearly twenty years. You may well remember how unsettling it was for me to watch Elizabeth Taylor go through a similar experience at relatively the same time — the difference being that her illnesses were public. I was, as far as the world was concerned, not alive. So there was not a moment in those twenty years that I could have gathered the emotional energy to make contact with someone who I saw at the time as clearly being a part of my previous life. Nor did I want to do so. At that time, the threat of the past intruding on the present really was much too great.

When I did finally recover from my illness, had assumed my new life and had a liver that actually functioned, I tried to track him down. It was not that I thought anything might continue between us — I was beyond that. It had been too long and, of course, one can never, as they say, recreate the magic. I found him and was unsurprised to learn that he had become an agent. He never acted as my agent, and I was specifically looking for a partner who did *not* do that. I fantasize that this may have been the right career for him because he was both a great supporter and somewhat star-struck. But as I say, at the time when we were involved I was able to accept the fact that he could love *both* me and "the star."

Anyway, I can't really defend my relationship with him anymore, and I don't want to. He was a sweet, kind boy. But in my life a pattern recurs over and over again. You must be aware of it; I've talked about it so often. Perhaps your knowledge of it explains your reticence to actually openly dismiss my relationship with Mickey. We both know that my evil and manipulative bitch of a mother had, in her arsenal, a unique and powerful weapon: she exercised a sublime and incorrigible skepticism about any and all of my life partners. She ridiculed Vincente to such an extent that I didn't ever want the two of them to be in the same room. Why did she refuse to support her daughter's relationships? Because she was intimidated by my talent and couldn't resist hoping that my life was merely a substandard imitation of her own. I'll never forget when, during my fifties comeback, after much nagging from Sid, I invited her to see my act at the Palace. She told Sid she didn't want to go. When he asked her why, she said, "Because at those concerts all anyone cares about is my daughter. They don't pay any attention to me." Is there any other mother who acted so consistently *unlike* a mother?

What she did, among other things, was make it virtually impossible for me to have a relationship. When in love I was habitually seized by twin and equally destructive emotions. On the one hand, I felt unworthy of any sort of love — she certainly taught me that. And simultaneously

I felt that the person I was in love with was unworthy of me. One might think these contradictory impulses would cancel each other out, but no, it was a perpetual seesaw. Which was it to be? Was I worthless or too worthy?

So when you even glancingly criticize Mickey — or make what in your letter proves to be a pathetic and obvious attempt to cover up your contempt for him and skepticism about our relationship — it touches me in a deep, angry place. It touches me where all my relationships are being ridiculed by my evil bitch of a mother. Shall we just call her the EBOAM? That sounds suitably and chillingly biblical, does it not?

Your analysis fails similarly in its attempt to understand the effects of drug addiction. I am not denying that I was a serious addict. I was *the* addict beyond all addicts. I was fully incapacitated, in terms of the ordinary faculties required to commit myself to certain tasks — remembering how to put one foot in front of the other, for instance. People were shocked at my onstage collapses. They had no idea of what transpired during a nightly binge. For even when I was so very wrecked onstage, it was, quite literally, nothing in comparison to my condition when I was off. I do not deny it. And I will not ever forget what it was like to be so seriously physiologically incapacitated by the poison I was pouring into my system.

On the other hand, it's important to note something that you could never know — because of your lack of experience — but can hopefully grow to understand. The drug addict does not, in the grip of his or her intoxication, become another person. Instead, they ultimately become more like themselves. It's like dying. June Allyson was a perfect example. I, of course, had no communication with her during her final years, but I did quietly observe her appearances on television.

I noted, for example, that she had become a success as a salesperson for urine-soaked underpants. This was the ultimate irony, that a person whose life had been devoted to jealously criticizing others had found a career as a spokesperson for a garment whose sole purpose was to collect human waste decorously, in a socially acceptable way. FYI: nowhere in those Depends ads did you ever see the words *adult diaper*. I shouldn't talk; indeed, I have worn many a diaper in my time. I have become, in effect, a piece of human waste in my old age. But nevertheless the irony of her terminal gig, as it were, was not lost on me. One of her final statements to the press contained a veiled reference to me. You may say I am sensitive to the point of paranoia, but be that as it may ... The Allyson leopard — she never changed her spots — talked of "the many tragic victims of show business." Apparently she was not one of them. In other words, the old cunt remained a prime bitch to the end.

The moral? People don't change when they die. They don't suddenly become kind and loving before the end. A bitch in life? A bitch she will remain. And in death, perhaps even more so. It is the same with drugs. Their effect is not to change us into better or worse people. Of course, we may stumble, stagger and even momentarily forget who and where we are. But if a person has no self-esteem, then a good old-fashioned booze binge, for instance — though it may lend the drinker a momentary dash of bravado — will ultimately lead her into a bottomless pit of self-doubt. For some this may even end in suicide.

And the same is true of all drugs. Their physiological effects may differ, but you don't become a different person. You simply become more of what you are. Sometimes the drug takes the infinitesimal seeds of some tendency and exaggerates them. This is why some people perceive that a drug has changed someone into another person. But the seed must be an integral part of the person if the drug is going to find it and exaggerate its effect.

I could not have fallen in love with Mickey because I was high. This simply doesn't happen. It could not have been that my clouded vision caused me to spend the last six months of my previous life as another person. I would have wished to find Mickey — on or off the drugs. On the drugs I happened, happily, to find him. And that is that. If all this is not enough to convince you that my reaction to a small comment from a woman with a cantilevered face is not a signal of an impending dire situation — and certainly these days it seems like nothing will do the trick — then let's try something else.

I think discussing your response to my analysis of Dash's papers might support my argument. What you seem to be hanging on to, and worrying over — the way a dog worries about an old bone — are the dangerous similarities between myself and Dash. I have given you scholarly justifications for my interest in his work. I'm not suggesting they are necessarily good arguments — and certainly far from the quality of what might be put in any academic paper — but they are nevertheless my considered thoughts. I took a lot of time thinking them through; they are sincere. In other words, I care about Dash because of the implications of his tragic life for twentieth-century theory.

Let's face it, most of the significant post-structuralists were homosexuals. Barthes, Foucault — importantly also Deleuze and Guattari. True, not Derrida — but every rule has its exception. It is interesting, and often ignored, that the collapse of homosexuality and the discreditation of theory (the rise of post-theory) occurred simultaneously, near the beginning of this century. Could the two have been connected? As I attempted to theorize in my last email, albeit ineptly, was there perhaps an association between the tragic arc of Dash King's life and the decline of post-structuralism? They may have both died of the same affliction: a fantastical irrelation to reality.

What I don't need from you now is a categorical dismissal of my ideas. Why have you not even addressed them? It is not that I am hurt. We don't have that kind of relationship and hopefully never will. Why ruin everything with scholarly etiquette? But it does disturb me that you don't engage with the extensive arguments I have made. Do they not seem, increasingly, to be relevant? This is what concerns me — along with your mentioning again that it's important that I'm *prepared*. (For what?) These elliptical remarks frighten me, of course. But what frightens me most is that it is very unlike you *not* to engage in what could prove to be a significant ideological discussion.

Do I need to spell it out for you? Nothing really has stepped into the breach to take over where theory and post-structuralism once reigned. There is the ever-perplexing transhuman philosophy, but this is, in my view, simply a rebranded version of post-structuralism (where the natural, real universe is not shaped by language, as the post-structuralists suggest, but instead by a future in which reality as we know it is, simply, old-fashioned, because we no longer exist in our bodies). I've always found this repellant. I fear that perhaps you're becoming a convert. Every time I ask you about your opinions on this, you change the subject. It is becoming increasingly clear that you will also change the subject when I talk about the death of post-structuralism in relation to Dash King. So I will not make another argument here. I have exhausted my arguments and I am insulted — not on an academic but on a pragmatic level — that you didn't respond. I will present you, instead, with more evidence for my previous argument: that

Dash's decline is a significant metaphor for the decline of an entire era.

But also, I think it's very important that you notice my attitude to Dash's spiralling fortunes. For instance, you comment on the fact that Dash's pathetic fate was to be romantically involved with a boy he seemed obsessed with on some manic/romantic level. Someone with whom he had nothing in common and with whom he couldn't have sex. It was a classic case of "mad love" — beyond even, or not relevant to, the "demon lover" syndrome, because, after all, Dash's lover simply did not have enough personality to be a demon.

But then you suggest I am interested in Dash because his neurotic relationships are somehow like mine. You don't come out and say it, but it seems you are implying that some or all of my lovers were inadequate, or that my relationships with them were mad. You also seem to think my lovers were also ciphers who, like Dash's lover, were too emotionally inadequate to be given the demon moniker. I hope this is not what you mean to suggest — though I think it is. I won't go there. I have just explained how horrible I find this condescension (or anyone's condescension) towards my romantic life. And why it disgusts me.

But the fact is I don't emulate Dash or idolize him — I analyze him. I certainly don't romanticize him. This is something you consistently imply, but you have no proof. I can see only one possible similarity between my romantic life and Dash's. The sole similarity (and this is me really searching . . . searching) is that Dash obviously prefers partners who are somewhat remote, who are ultimately inaccessible. What was the term in my time? Oh yes, people who were "emotionally distant." This is certainly the type of partner I always preferred. But I think that tendency is adequately explained by the boundary issues that were created by my mother.

However, there is no equivalency here. Dash was emotionally abused by a young man who treated him very badly. This is classic homosexual masochism. This is not something I have experienced or wanted to experience. A little distance is enough for me; outright cruelty is taking things a bit too far. The reason I would like you to examine the writing below is that Dash talks, in his own sad way, about the effects that fame had on him. The whole idea of such a small-time theatre artist in a one-horse Canadian town being obsessed with the effects of fame on his short, though melodramatic, life is . . . amusing.

Again, I think you can see — especially in my response — that I have no personal investment in Dash. I am distanced from his agonies. Dash was a kind of Samson Agonistes — or, at any rate, saw himself that way.

I see Dash's obsession with fame as humorous because he wrote during his — what seems to us exceedingly short — lifetime perhaps fifty plays. They were occasionally produced. By himself, I might add. They were also occasionally celebrated — mainly by politically correct people who were trying to be nice. They were considered shocking for the post-Victorian sensibility that peaked before the turn of the last century. People still had the capacity to be upset by gay plays. Gay actually *meant* something. Dash's demonization at the hands of the public and academia — at least, according to himself — ultimately led to his suicide. Dash's papers indicate this. And it was certainly suicide: death from a heart attack induced by extreme overuse of amyl nitrates — poppers.

In the passage below we find Dash in the throes of agony over what he says is his academic humiliation. Academia was evidently where he went to escape his lack of success in the theatre world. (Nothing short of world renown would have satisfied his narcissism!) In the end, it is to this world of fame obsession that Dash retreats. He becomes possessed by his ostracism, of what he perceives as his enormous, hugely underrated talent. His later papers are to some degree all about fame. This, again, is ironic. Dash was no Marlene Dietrich — he only imagined himself to be. It's important that you understand I am not emulating Dash for his insane megalomania. I do not wish I were Dash. Nor do I — lady with the cantilevered face or not — wish I was famous again.

Here is Dash. Brace yourself; it's not pretty.

Antonio:
I guess you know the latest. All of you academic types know what's going on with each other all the time, don't you? I mean you probably knew about my journal article being rejected before I did, didn't you? I'm so fucking pissed off right now it's hard not to be pissed off with you too. You are the most fucking sympathetic heterosexual I ever met. How's that for a compliment? But I've had it. I'm not casting these pearls before swine anymore. My whole artistic life has been about that. I'm a very funny guy, you know. I could have written for TV. I could have done any sort of writing for money. But instead I decided to write for theatre because I believed in gay liberation. Once! Not anymore. Not now — now that none of the faggots ever want to see this old drag queen's irrelevant plays. You're just a sympathetic liberal. You don't know how savage the gay community can be. Take my word for it — they're a bunch of wild animals. They tear apart their young, and

that means any member of their community that becomes rich and famous. I was only famous for a while, and it practically killed me. I'm still suffering from the effects.

So *Queer Studies* has rejected my piece on drag. This is after they accepted it, and the journal went to print (but without my article). It's the last straw. I've had it with the whole fucking lot of you. You're all a bunch of pinched assholes, your mouths are little pinched assholes and you're so insanely focused on your fucking career trajectories that each and every one of you takes pride in stamping out any point of view you disagree with, or that might threaten yours. I assume you know that I was pushing the idea that drag was transhistorical? Yes, my article had the temerity to suggest that maybe there were drag queens in the Early Modern era. I was nuts to even think about suggesting such a thing. The powers that be won't have it. The academic line they're all toeing is "Foucault says that homosexuality was invented by Oscar Wilde in the late nineteenth century so how could there be drag queens in 1580?" Of course, no one would dare question Foucault. Never that.

But what makes me maddest is not the rejection — although that was pretty amazing. Some heavy-duty backstage politics must be going on. I mean, the editor accepted the piece and then a month went by and then some mysterious second reader decided to drop it. Then there is the rejection phrase. I'll never forget it. The reader who cut my article thought my argument about drag was not "sufficiently nuanced." Fuck, after nearly thirty years of doing gay theatre and being a drag queen, and after three years of reading a bunch of damn boring theory books and fucking tedious histories of Renaissance theatre (why do we have to call it fucking Early Modern; can't we just call it the Renaissance?), my argument isn't sufficiently *nuanced*? I'll tell you what happened. They didn't want this drag queen writing for an academic journal. I mean, they at first thought they did. For a while. They started out by thinking it would be great to have a real drag queen's point of view. Instead of the usual, academics talking about drag queens, they finally get a real one to talk about herself. But when they actually have to read an essay by a fucking drag queen — an essay that sounds like typical academic crap, but hey, I can't hide it, is actually from the heart — well, they can't handle that. I mean, wow, the piece might actually have some truth in it. I guess I just don't do enough academicspeak to hide that truth.

This is why I'm leaving academia and why I left the theatre. Everybody hates me because I'm too gay. I've always been *too* everything. Now I'm *too* gay. When I came out, people believed being gay was being a girly boy and a pansy and confronting the patriarchy. Now that's old-fashioned. Nobody wants to see a gay play or read a gay poem. So I figured I'd become a gay academic. I mean, everybody's doing queer theory, right? But I'm too late. I didn't get in in time to escape the latest academic bulldozer. You know — postgender, transgender. Because I haven't had a sex change I'm actually behind the times. Hey, you know, I wish they said they were rejecting my paper simply because it was dated. There's a lot of resentment in that word, *nuanced*. Let's face it, these guys know who wrote it. I mean, the article may be submitted blind, but they can find out. People know I'm going to school here, and that I'm a triple threat: a writer, director and academic. *They can't hack it.* I'm the real thing. I know you think I'm becoming unbalanced. It's pretty interesting that you said you are uncomfortable with how personal I am getting. Isn't that the point? Isn't that the gist? Academics can't ever be personal.

Hey, I've got news for you — scholarly stuff *is* personal. That high-toned, distanced jargon they use is just there to hide the fact that it's all about personalities. They've got the same petty jealousies, the same plotting and planning behind the scenes, as other flawed humans. You said in your phone message that I should stop sending you written messages because you want to talk to me in person. Or, you think I should see an academic counsellor.

Well, I'm not like ordinary people. I'm a famous faggot and I've been around this *too small* town too long. Do you know who the academic counsellor at the University of Toronto is? He's another faggot. Haven't you seen the little rainbow flags in his office? And he even has one that says, "Safe space for queers." Right, I would be *so* safe with him. I've met him a couple of times at academic gatherings. He's come right up and talked to me. *And* he indicated that if I needed any *help* he would be there. I know what this is all about. It's not about him getting in my pants — he just wants to have a famous patient. So I can't go to the school's academic counsellor because he's gay and I'm gay and I'm too fucking well-known. He wouldn't approve of me, anyway, because I'm such a slut. None of them do. Jesus Christ, I could *never* talk to him about my boyfriend. Most faggots think me being a slut is bad enough. If they knew how fucked-up my relationship with my boyfriend is they'd never forgive me. I'm sure the good counsellor would want me to dump my reason to live. Sometimes I think the beautiful boy is also my reason to die. The good counsellor would advise me to get a boyfriend who was old and fat and sensible.

Shakespeare would understand what I'm going through. He understood it all in those damn sonnets. Love doesn't make sense. And I can only see a gay psychologist, because if I were to tell the details of my promiscuous life to a straight one they would have me locked up in a nanosecond. But the gay psychologists always want me to fall in love with some doctor or lawyer type. Isn't that funny? Some professional guy. Well, I know two gay doctors who are married. They are HIV positive and both on heavy-duty AIDS drugs. They also like to do a lot of non-prescription pharmaceuticals that they get for free from pharmaceutical reps. They do these drugs when they're having unsafe sex with their HIV-positive friends at the sex parties they have once every week in their living room. Oh yeah, I should find myself a nice *respectable* doctor and get married.

The world is coming to an end. I know because I'm watching it fall apart around me. Maybe it's just my world that's ending. Maybe that's what suicide is. Don't worry, people who really end up committing suicide don't talk about it. Or do they? Have you heard about David Prent? Of course you've heard about him. I think what happened to David Prent is what's happening to the gay world. We are being erased and forgotten. Am I the last faggot? Is God trying to kill all of us? All the interesting ones, at least? I do think there's something to the idea that all the interesting ones died of AIDS — *because they did!* Only the mediocre, dumb fucks are left. And the mediocre dumb fucks are busy figuring out ways to procreate with dumb-fuck lesbians of the same ilk, so they can have mediocre dumb-fuck children and take over the world. Well, David Prent was a brilliant gay visual artist. And now he's brain-dead. And what are they saying happened? Oh yeah, an embolism. He had a brain embolism, and now he's lying in a hospital bed staring at the wall. That's nice. Good for him. But of course no one mentions the fact that he was a party boy, and liked to do party drugs.

Everyone is doing drugs and having unsafe sex these days, as if there is no AIDS. As if AIDS is over. Or maybe it's just that AIDS can't kill you the way it used to, so these guys choose to overdose on party drugs instead. You can't go to a bathhouse and get a legitimate fuck without someone trying to get you to try some Tina or just get right down and do crack. And all the nice dumb faggots try to keep up the fiction that we all like to stay home and knit with our husbands and our nice sexless lesbian friends. Well, drugs may become the cause of our demise but they aren't the reason. The reason is that the good Lord above has decided to rid the world of every single fag that ever lived. AIDS started the job, but there are still a few stragglers. Like David Prent. You know what David Prent was working on before his brain died? He was putting together a visual history of the asshole. He'd been working on it for about six years. And he just got a *huge* Canada Council grant. Do you believe that? From the Canada Council. And what was David going to say about the asshole with his artistic research? He was going to say it was important to world history. He was going to say that the asshole was a way of life. You know what Hocquenghem says? No. Nobody cares what Hocquenghem says these days — except for me. He says, "We're all women from behind." Well, David's artistic project was to build a little library dedicated to the asshole with all the materials he had collected about asshole fetishism. And this Museum of the Anus was going to be housed at Dalhousie University. And he was fabulous and feeling like all was perfect in his world. After all, he had the Canada Council and some crazy Maritime university behind him. Then, just like that, he had an embolism. I had met with him a couple of days before he went vegetative. He talked about how well his life was going. He had quite a bit of material for the Rectal Rectory: videos, sex toys, books, articles ... He was going to do them up all pretty. He told me there were a couple of huge rooms full of stuff. Then, *pffft!* The next day he's gone. What's going to happen to David's Butt Breviary? Dalhousie would have probably been too scared to display it anyway. But part of his Canada Council grant was to be paid to that university, so they couldn't very well say no. So, what will probably happen is the Asshole Library will sit somewhere in the bowels of Dalhousie, because the only person who was interested in it was David Prent. And now he's lost his wits. And no one else will touch his giant visual ode to the asshole with a ten-foot pole.

I'm going drinking tonight. And after that I'm going to do lots of poppers. I'm going to get lots of strange boys who remind me of my boyfriend to sit on my face. Sometimes I can imagine it's *him* sitting on my face. That's the closest thing I know to love. My boyfriend even said that he may never pee on me again. Who cares? I'll have a nice night out. And maybe I'll die in the hot tub. That's where I'd really like to die, with the smell of some strange boy's butt in my lips. Some butt that makes me cry — because I can imagine it's the butt of the boy who will never love me the way I want to be loved. Oh, by the way, if I do die, can you tell that nice lady that edited the journal that I just wasn't "nuanced" enough for this life? I'd really appreciate that.

Dash's melodrama suits his personality and his career. His plays are filled with screaming drag queens and pathetic dramaturgical attempts to create real female characters, who are of course nothing but drag queens themselves. Thank God the drag queens don't do me anymore. It was a kind of homage. But ultimately it became fromage. Am I being flip enough for you? Dash King was a footnote to history — if that. Like all those at the beginning of this century who were still flogging identity politics and bemoaning its demise, he became obsolete. But even this passage — where he bemoans the death of David Prent's dream — is symbolic of an era. It is an era of extreme self-delusion. This is a man who believed that Shakespeare was not Shakespeare. He could also convince himself that he was exemplifying the masochism of Shakespeare's sonnets by remaining in a sick, loveless relationship. He was a man who relished the ultimate humiliation. He routinely searched for the aroma of the anus of the man he loved in the anus of strangers. In terms of Dash King, there is no "there" there. This is only a lost soul who has left reality behind.

My theory is that he involved himself so deeply in identity politics that he lost any sense of who he actually was or what he wanted. The narrative he fell into (like Alice down the rabbit hole) was that he would be a tragic figure and suffer for his love. Is this not something like Baudrillard's hyperreal? Baudrillard's notion that Disneyland was America — was that not a particularly camp, homosexual notion? How much reality is there in valourizing a library devoted to the asshole — except as a futile reaction against the reality of the homophobia he was all too powerless to defy? Yet Dash's obsession with identity made the whole situation even worse than it might have been.

Is it not possible that post-structuralism itself is just, in its intellectual reality, a bunch of fags denying that any "there" is there? Remember that Gertrude Stein, a very gay lesbian, invented that catchy phrase. Well, Gertrude and the fags that followed her have been desperately trying to convince the heterosexual world that their lives had transcended that fantasy. They fervently hoped that marriage and traditional families — which they were excluded from at the time — were constructs.

Dash despised Foucault for, it seems to me, very silly reasons: identity politics mostly. But he would find my critique of Foucault homophobic. It's too bad he can't come back from the grave to argue with me. I would say, "Relax; have sex with whoever you want. If you had lived long enough, like me, you would be able to do that. In the future, in cyberspace, all things are possible."

Listen, I want to tell you something. It's a minor thing, very minor. It's not really related to my analysis. But, of course, I must tell you everything.

I remember looking for an analyst during my "comeback." My first therapist was in awe of me — much in the way that Dash imagines that therapists are in awe of him. But Dash shows his superficiality and banality when he suggests that he couldn't have a therapist because he was too famous for one. On the contrary, Dash's actual lack of fame was his big disappointment — but one he would never own up to. He was not internationally famous, so there would have been no reason for a psychoanalyst, psychologist or therapist of any ilk to be in awe of him. But it's more than that. Analysts are *only* in awe of great people. I'm not saying that I am great, in the sense of being an amazing talent. Although it's true some people seem to think I am. I can't think of myself that way, of course. And shouldn't. And don't ever now. But there is such a thing as a "great" person — and by that I mean large. That is what I always was — too large for this world. Dash suggests that he was too much. But that too-muchness — this can be gleaned from his letters — is easily contained. It is even more easily parodied.

On the contrary, some of the therapists I visited literally ran from me, frightened, tails between their legs. I had one lock me out of his office. True, I was high on something at the time. I thought it was very funny when it happened; we got into an argument and I just wouldn't let up. I had to have it out with him. He was terrified. This didn't have anything to do with me being famous. It had everything to do with me being "great" — not just a little "too much," but *really too much for this world.*

Anyway, my very first therapist said something I will never forget. I think I was worried because Sid, in his effort to support a cleaned-up but very obese version of moi, desperately wanted to know everything about me. He endeavoured to peer into every corner of my life. And, at the time, that included searching my chest of drawers.

Yes, I kept a little stash of uppers in a bra — one I never wore because it was way too tight. The bra had been a functioning part of my wardrobe when I was way too skinny. I asked the doctor rather ingenuously if Sid had the right to look in my drawers simply because he was my husband. I remember he smiled indulgently. Little did he know that, with every word he said, he was enabling my overpowering addiction. I could find enablement anywhere. He said to me, "In every marriage, there is something that is hidden between two people. My father was a very mild-mannered, quiet sort of person, who was dominated by my mother." (Another one of my special talents — I could always get a therapist to end up telling me his troubles instead of listening to mine. I certainly didn't deliberately try to turn the tables on them, but I am very sympathetic, I have a good sense of humour and I love people. Therapists are so attracted to and intimidated by me that they find it more comfortable, ultimately, to talk about themselves.) He went on: "And my mother really did control my father, and he was very quiet and passive. But after he died we did find some things hidden in the closet, something that belonged to my father that none of us, even my mother, knew about."

It was an ancient, tiny knife.

We all must have something that is simply ours, something that is just private. Yes, even my therapist's mother's henpecked husband had private places. But I cannot hide anything from you. It's all open. This has much to do with the fact that long ago you accepted me unconditionally. I will never forget that. For someone like me — who never knew unconditional love — receiving it, finally, is utterly overwhelming. And even though our romance was never sexual, it might as well have been. I really do wish I was a lesbian, or was lesbianic — a more proper twenty-first-century appellation. No, I must tell you everything. And what I am going to say — I'm sure it will irritate you. But isn't that what happens when people love, even if they don't have sex with each other? But you will always come back. I know you will. Anyway, this is the small thing. I don't know how you could not think it small. I don't know how we could be that out of sync.

Allworth convinced me to take another trip to the Tranquility Spa.

You are right to suggest he is a bad influence. This is something I remember from so long ago. Boys — usually homosexuals — always love to indulge my every whim because they are in love with me. Or my fame. Allworth is not in love with my fame, though he knows of it. But I think he finds me divinely entertaining. He gave me that sly look and, to his credit, that sly look absolutely gives me permission to say no. There was a little giggle. "Would you like to go again to the Tranquility Spa?" At first I said, "I don't think so." And he said, "That's fine, I don't want to force the idea on you. I have no reason to go there and no reason to take you there. I simply thought you might want to go." And I could see that he really was thinking of my feelings, which immediately made me realize I wasn't being judged or pressured. "You know, I don't think I would mind going again," I said.

I don't know why I agreed to go. Perhaps it was just that Allworth was so easygoing. And not only didn't I feel pressured, but I also didn't feel observed. It is one of the things that makes me sure that Allworth isn't star-struck. I mean, he is, somewhat. But star-struck isn't his ultimate attitude. I simply delight him. I wish I was more attracted to him, but I'm not. (For, as you know, I'm quite capable of persuading even the most recalcitrant homo to submit to my lips.) I think he might have sex with me, though he prefers men. I think he would have sex with anyone, especially if it was someone he liked. And if he thought it would please them.

You know, for some people, offering sex is like offering coffee or dessert. That's what so many don't understand. Sex was often like that for me. Other people — those like June Allyson — offered more innocent fare: a hot-cross bun or candy from a pink dish. I offered blow jobs. I didn't then, nor do I now, find my behaviour abhorrent or disgusting. In fact, I find people who don't understand the sheer practicality of sex simply rude. It is, after all, a bodily function. Many a man was nonplussed by the suggestion of fellatio — partly because women aren't supposed to do such a thing. But you know, it often happens. And once they get over the novelty of my taking the initiative, they can breathe a sigh of relief. What would happen if sex was as normal as eating? Being guilty about sex makes as much sense as being guilty about an eating binge. These days there is no reason to be guilty. There are too many solutions: the fat can be sucked out; a pill can make the pounds disappear. And it is rare that anything we eat is *actually* fattening. Ingeniously, food just looks and tastes that way now. So why feel guilty? "Oh, I've just done a terrible thing . . . I've eaten." But eating is something we all need to do. But then there's: "I've just done a horrible thing, I've given a man a blow job as routinely as June Allyson might have offered him a croissant." Don't these statements seem ridiculous?

Allworth understands this, even though we haven't talked about it in so many words. We do discuss sex. That is, he enjoys relating his exploits without bragging or being distasteful. He talks filth, but he does not aggrandize himself. Sexual anecdotes only disgust me if they smell of boasting. So it was easy to say yes to Allworth's suggestion that we return to the Tranquility Spa. Allworth is also very indulgent about how long it takes me to get out of the house and into a cab. And what I really value is that he continues talking to me even when people are horrified or unduly perturbed by my shape. At least when I'm with him I forget momentarily the horror that is my appearance. I had taken the liberty of wearing a little black dress. It was, in fact, a Chanel. They are timeless, of course, but it's something I usually don't dare wear. Not because the dress is revealing — rather because it seems a little presumptuous for something so ugly to encase itself in something so beautiful.

When we entered the Tranquility Spa all was casual; no one took any notice of us. As per usual we were not the most grotesque beings present. I recognized some of the old crowd. The woman with the cantilevered face was in her usual place, chatting up the nippleless bartender whose gender we had not yet determined. (I know we're not supposed to care — but we still wonder, don't we?) Off in a corner, the handless man was nursing a drink in a bowl. He was pushing it about on the table with his stumps. Now and then he would dip his head and lap at it ... It was very sad. As I sat down at the bar with Allworth, I thought of how easy it might be for the Handless Man if the Cantilevered Lady were to sit down with him. After all, she could lift the bowl and pour it. But it was not to be that simple. Life, human relationships, are not that simple. It's not simply about getting a hand when you need one. Unfortunately, there is shame, repulsion, revulsion and sexual *preference*. And the Cantilevered Lady is a handful, pardon the pun. This is almost preposterously evident.

As we slowly made our way from the door to the bar, the dilemma was whether or not to sit close to the Cantilevered Lady. If we were to sit beside her, it would seem too familiar, an invitation to discussion. If we were to sit too far away, it might be viewed as insulting. I chose a seat about halfway down the bar. Allworth, recognizing that I had forged a solution to this sticky predicament, helped me into my chair.

Once I got there I happened to glance at the door to the backroom. I noticed that the Doll Boy was standing there, doing nothing really — looking rather listless. There was a creature sitting at another table, all alone, at the other end of the room. It was not easy to see this creature because of the lighting. This made me want to swivel myself in the chair, for the angle at which I was sitting offered an indirect view. But once I have sat, as you well know, there is very little possibility of me actually wriggling around. The creature seemed to be male. But, as I say, there is no telling how any of these creatures started out. He seemed a neutral sort of figure. His movements were neutral as he pulled the glass to his face and sipped. The light was falling over him in such a way that he constantly moved in and out of it. In fact, the light was flashing off him. I couldn't help looking at him again and again. But if the creature had caught me, it wouldn't have mattered, because the angle at which I was seated veiled the fact that I was staring. After a moment or two, I realized he had two faces.

It would be more accurate to say that his face was divided in two. I noticed this because he would turn his head to take a drink and look to the side; but there was nothing to look at, so I was suspicious of this movement.

When he did this, different parts of his face would hit the light. This was clearly an unfinished plastic-surgery job. One side of his face was perfect and the other looked like a barely congealed mass of ground chuck. It was hard to discern anything on the ground-chuck side. There was a lump where the side of his nose should have been. The other side of his face was perfect. But not in the way the Doll Boy's face was perfect. It was not seamless, not smooth and plastic, but instead perfectly human. It looked just like a real face. Was it possible that one half of his face had been dipped in battery acid and not the other? Well, why then could they not fix it? I had heard of instances where people had so many plastic surgeries that they became allergic to it — that their bodies rejected the chemicals that were inserted in them. Perhaps this was what had happened to him. Because it was as if a line had been drawn down the middle of his face, and one half of his face had been fixed, while the other had not.

After I had figured out what was going on, I looked back at Allworth, and realized I had been staring. But to his credit, he didn't chide me. I could see that he thought my interest in the lone creature at the table was a typical human reaction, and he forgave me for it. I wanted to make a remark about the creature's face just so Allworth would understand what was obsessing me. For Allworth couldn't see it from where he was sitting. But I'm sure he knew — even if he couldn't clearly see the creature's half-face — why I was staring.

I tried to remember that my own appearance was certainly more disgusting and off-putting than the visage of this creature who had perhaps become immune to plastic surgery. I was, after all, a creature for whom plastic surgery was hopeless. As you know, my bones are now so brittle they could not take any sort of bruising. So I am simply a living, breathing demonstration of human disintegration in all its glory.

His half-face reminded me of the mask worn by the Phantom of the Opera. I remember when I was recovering from one of my liver operations, in Dubai (the successful one), I woke up in a hospital bed. There was an episode of *Entertainment Tonight* on TV that featured scenes from *The Phantom of the Opera* — the hit megamusical at the time. I was experiencing one of those odd, dreamlike moments that you always remember. I was half awake and half asleep, very much in pain, and powerless to correct my condition. The scenes from *The Phantom of the Opera* seemed to be taking a terribly long time. They kept repeating themselves, over and over. I remember John Tesh or Mary Hart saying, "This play is going to revolutionize musical theatre." I remember being vaguely interested (in my gormless state) because, of course, I myself had something to do with the development of the American musical when I was young. What, after all, might have been revolutionary at such a late date? I don't remember anything more about the program except that it became nightmarish to watch — and that it made me anxious. I do remember leaving both the hospital and Dubai, many months later, and asking someone — a male nurse who was taking care of me — about *The Phantom of The Opera*. The inveterate old fag said, "It was all stolen from Puccini and it destroyed musical theatre." I didn't really understand. But it seemed a shame.

All this was running through my mind. And then, before I knew it, the Cantilevered Lady was sitting next to me. She had sprinted over from the other end of the bar. She was remarkably limber — though doubtless very old with that wreck of a face. So I was now sitting between her and Allworth. This was an impossible situation. Her comment the last time about "the man that got away" had made me very insecure. And it had been made about the Handless Man, who was now ignoring her. Was she *so very* unappealing as a person — beyond her deformity — or were they just not suited to each other? Well, anyway, there was something about her I didn't like. Unfortunately, it was *not* her face. Her face certainly appalled me, but only in the way one is appalled by a car accident. That's not hatred or moral judgement, just a visceral response. No, what appalled me was that I realized immediately she was a slimy character. It's the kind of thing one realizes all too quickly. This is partly, or even completely, because she pretended immediately that we were intimate.

This is perhaps the most repellent of human tendencies. I certainly experienced it when I was a star and I was never left unfazed. People would walk up to me and address me by my Hollywood name. I would turn out of politeness, and they would proceed, chatting away about their dogs or the weather. It really was amazing *and* frightening. They would then proceed to use my Hollywood name over and over, as if they were practising it, or savouring it, or, even more alarming, masturbating with it. I often felt the urge to yank out the hoary old phrase "That's my name, don't wear it out!" But, of course, my Hollywood name wasn't my name at all. Invariably the chat would be of the most mundane variety. It was as if it were a test. "How long will it be before she breaks, bolts or just plain hits me?" Yes, certainly, incidents like this were expected — part of the job. But surely they knew that I was caught, trapped, because it *was* my job, and therefore I could not simply ignore them. Of course they knew, and they took cruel advantage. And on top of that, I was *such* a good little MGM girl. So I would just smile and search desperately for any means of escape.

The Cantilevered Lady began chatting in a similar familiar fashion (but, thankfully, without using my old star name) as soon as she was beside me. She spoke as if we were, in fact, in mid-conversation, as if we had only been cut off momentarily and were now back on track. She leaned into me intimately and whispered. It was disconcerting. I was worried she might wound me with part of her face. She spoke in a drunken tone. Allworth could not hear her little diatribe. He looked at us curiously, not sure if I had found a new friend or an irritating pest.

I couldn't believe what she was saying. She began by pointing part of her face in the direction of the Man with Two Faces. I suppose she thought this was more polite than pointing a finger, but there was really no difference. "Get a load of him," she said — or words to that effect. There was definitely something of the truck driver's moll about her, faintly reminiscent of Ida Lupino in *They Drive by Night*. "Can you believe it?" she said, referring to the poor man's face. "What kind of accident was that?"

I was truly appalled. Such situations are always very difficult for me, because I am, essentially, a nice person. I never want to be rude. So I smiled and nodded and even perhaps laughed with her. But it hurts for me to laugh. So I did not, thankfully, laugh too hard. I think Allworth recognized I was uncomfortable. But he didn't know what to do. Of course she kept going on and on — she was not the type to speak briefly or worry about taking up too much of your time.

As she continued, I began to think about the horrors of humanity — even to the point of pondering the Holocaust. It seemed to me that she was a person who was ultimately and pathetically *human*; someone who epitomized mankind's grossest evil. You see, though she was perhaps, other than myself, the ugliest creature on earth, she could not pass up this opportunity to make fun of someone who might possibly be perceived as less fortunate. She was not merely condescending to, or pathologizing, the creature in the corner; ultimately she was dehumanizing him.

And is this not, ironically, what it means to be human? Aristotle suggested that it was our ability to learn, or our capacity to reason, that ultimately separates humans from animals. But is it really that? And surely it's not just opposable thumbs! I would suggest, instead, that what makes us fully human is, paradoxically, our tendency to treat fellow human beings as if they were animals. Or worse. We love animals, and pity them in a way we do not pity other human beings. Perhaps one should say it is our ability to treat other human beings as if they were rocks or stones. Whatever tragedy had befallen the Man with Two Faces, nothing could be crueller, especially in the Tranquility Spa, of all places, than to make fun of him. The woman's jibes obviously forced a comparison: "He is so much worse off than I am."

What is it? Do we so fear death that we must wish it upon others? Are we so superstitious that we imagine misfortune is like a malignant spell that might waft from someone else upon us? Is the only way to protect ourselves, therefore, to put a safe distance between ourselves and the "other" with mockery? Why does it invariably make us feel better to cause other people pain? Of course, my mother's heartless, unrelenting sternness in that room in San Gabriel is very much on my mind here.

I didn't know what to do; I had to get away. If I continued smiling and nodding, which was my deeply inadequate *modus operandi*, she might have gone on all night. Perhaps she might have slipped into pantomime, fully visible to her poor victim, and acted out her condescension and ridicule. I turned to Allworth and said, "Where is the washroom?" Of course, he knew at once this was a ruse, that I had to get away from the woman beside me.

We couldn't simply leave — we had only just walked in. It seemed like the only solution. He pointed to a door in the centre of the wall opposite where the Handless Man and the Man with Two Faces were sitting. I am not capable of going to the bathroom in the way normal people do, in a public convenience. But there was no way this vicious, boring creature could have known that. I would just hide in the bathroom and wait until I came up with a better plan. Perhaps Allworth could tell her that I had been ill and we had to leave.

This plan was forming as Allworth offered to assist me in the complex process of disembarking from my stool, but I waved him away. It occurred to me that a couple of minutes alone with that monster would make what had compelled me to leave all too clear.

When I reached the washroom, the door was remarkably light. Was it made of paper? A good thing, at any rate, as I am very weak. Inside was like nothing I could have imagined. It's been a long time since I used a public washroom. And, of course, it has been many years since they abolished gender-specific toilets. I never seem to get used to the neutral streamlined atmospheres that are the typical twenty-first-century washroom environment. I long for the antique powder rooms — the baroque mirrors and makeup tables, comfortable chairs, curtains and attendants. There is nothing like that now. But it struck me as odd that the washroom was so very dark. Then suddenly it made sense. Obviously — although the backroom was "arranged" for people to have sex — it was the washroom where people more routinely consummated their assignations.

The room smelled heavenly, a mixture of cinnamon and coconut. A soothing music played. A laser light was aimed at the ceiling, shooting straight up from the floor beside the sink. It did not illuminate anything, just cast a pale blue. I made my way towards one of the two cubicles because it occurred to me that I might be able to gather my wits there. And I thought that perhaps the toilet seat might be low enough for me to perch on, not too uncomfortably. But before I reached the door, I noticed a movement beside the other cubicle — in a slender space between it and the wall. I took a few steps over and glanced into a sort of side area.

Standing against the wall in the corner was the Doll Boy. This was simply where he was. It wasn't as if it was natural for him to be there, but it certainly looked as if it was usual. And he was naked — from the waist down. His pants were in a little puddle on the floor. I couldn't help thinking about Dash King's poignant reference to the puddle he was allowed to make on his boyfriend's thigh. The Doll Boy looked amazing. Beautiful is perhaps not an accurate term. Although he was, technically, beautiful, the odd thing about him was that he could not really *be* beautiful because he was so obviously fake. But the fact that his skin resembled the surface of a modern plastic item, perhaps an airliner or an automobile (only, of course, more pliable), did not mean that he was not, technically, perfectly formed.

My surprise was more of a pragmatic kind. For though I was surprised to see him, it seemed somehow inevitable. He was offering himself — not to me, of course — but to any monster who might happen to wander into the washroom from the bar. No, I was surprised because it had been such a long time since I put myself in a situation where I might offer a man a blow job. In fact, it has been nearly sixty years. And back then I was certainly not as slumped over as I am now. Sixty years ago I was not in this depressing curlicue, and had only just begun to suffer from bad knees. Back then when I contemplated giving a man a blow job, I was taken aback by the anticipation of cracking joints — the pain, the sounds, the *awkwardness*.

Too much. But imagine my surprise to realize I am, in fact, now the perfect height to offer a blow job to a perfectly formed man (someone like the Doll Boy, who is, I would say, approximately six feet tall).

And there it was, in front of me. The Doll Penis. It was not, I immediately noted, particularly large or small. I was amazed at the detail. It was uncircumcised. Obviously it had been fashioned by a superior, loving artisan, a stellar plastic surgeon who loved penises very much. This appendage must have been his crowning achievement. There was something Davidish about it. What is the essence of Michelangelo's *David*? As many have remarked, it is the epitome of youthful, coiled energy, the shaft resting so gently on the testicles, like a cobra disdaining the impulse to strike, brutally cognizant of its latent power.

It is important for you to take note of what I did next. I gazed at the Doll Boy's penis, somewhat dispassionately, musing over the practical possibility of an erection. Since the Doll Boy's entire body was encased in a kind of plastic, would it be possible for him to manage it? Wouldn't it rip the casing? There are men who experience a condition called paraphimosis, where the glans gets trapped behind the skin, and they cannot experience an erection. It was hard to imagine that the Doll Boy would have been afflicted with this, as there was something so perfect about the way his penis rested there. But was his plastic skin elastic?

Unfortunately, I couldn't manage to look at his face, as it would have been interesting to also see his expression, and whether his demeanour was as expectant as his appendage appeared to be. But in my crooked posture that would not have been possible. It was after a moment or two of this kind of contemplation that Allworth burst in. I was very happy to see him. He asked me if I was all right, and I said I was fine. And he then mentioned how appalling the Cantilevered Lady was, saying there was no getting rid of her. He whispered, "Should we leave?" And then tactifully added, "Or are you . . . busy?" Allworth is too well-mannered to have glanced at the Doll Boy's nakedness. I appreciated the notion that I might still be capable of a sexual encounter, but happily, not at all sadly, I shook my head. Allworth, once we left, was immediately apologetic. He was concerned about my welfare and not at all perturbed by the Doll Boy. I told him not to worry.

This visit to the Tranquility Spa had been a scientific experiment. It had gone exactly as I had imagined. Nothing overt had happened. I had not gone wild, or gotten extraordinarily drunk, or ended up finding someone who deals uppers (are there still such things?) and falling off the wagon. The grand finale of your imaginings would, of course, be me meticulously fellating a veritable chorus line of handsome men. But no, nothing like that occurred. You may be disappointed to hear that I simply visited a bona fide dive, that's all. I felt privileged to be able to observe the goings-on, to get out of my lair to see how the other half lives. Longing for an encounter of a sexual kind was irrelevant. I did not feel at all frustrated or disappointed that my contemplation of the Doll Boy had been interrupted. Indeed, it had been time to leave.

So that's the whole story. I hope you will not be too disappointed that I am not the reckless libertine you had perhaps imagined I was, or that I have proved once and for all that I can be trusted. You spend so much time warning me of the perils of my lifestyle. Does all this time spent curled up at home with my new, convenient integration, communicating with you re: Dash King's tragic legacy — with an occasional visit to the Tranquility Spa — constitute a lifestyle? I suppose it does, technically.

We waited until we had left the bar and passed by the

nice Asian woman maintaining the spa illusion at the front door — the wait was absolutely necessary due to the looming presence of the Cantilevered Lady — and then Allworth whispered to me that maybe it would be better to come back another time, perhaps when the Cantilevered Lady was not there. We both noted that this might prove an impossible plan as she seemed a permanent fixture. Allworth said that if we ever wanted to go back he could check to see if she was present first. But it made no difference to me (although it was sweet of him to care). It didn't matter if we returned or not; returning was the furthest thing from my mind.

Please know that I am not chiding you for your concern. I love it and, increasingly, I am able to see it as a sign of love. Just remember that for someone like me, who never received any proper love as a child, who only had a controlling mother, primarily interested in corralling her daughter for her own projects, it's not easy to accept admonitions. I know you aren't looking to control me for your own purposes, that you're just trying to help. The two actions look very much the same, but I know in my heart of hearts they are not. I want you to think of how addiction operates — the vacillations between abstinence and indulgence. I want you to think of what I am suggesting as my new lifestyle — a kind of consistent voyeurism, with no possibility of veering away, or of participating in any kind of indulgence. Still, you may not approve.

I am steeling myself for your response, whatever it may be. You know, one of my doctors, nearly twenty years ago (only a year after we first met), told me about the changes that had occurred in me after I met you. I wasn't even conscious of them. "You know," he offered, "you have always been just this side of a curmudgeon." He said this in the way that someone informs a person of something negative about their character, or the character of someone close to them, after the fact ("I never liked your husband"). It is not easy for me to imagine myself as a curmudgeon. But maybe someone who has lived so long and is so set in her opinions (if not her ways) might appear that way to the world at large. At any rate, you have perhaps saved me from becoming one. You have taught me how to bend and sway — an apt metaphor for someone who so resembles a crippled branch. I will never forget that, whatever our differences.

I s something missing? Something has changed in your tone. There are inconsistencies in your argument. Paradoxes even. This is so unlike you. I am not really angry, but I am feeling rebellious — *very* rebellious. This makes me less angry. It's like a child whose parents suddenly stop scolding him, when their reprimands become milder. Of course, this is just before they pull out the big guns: "You're grounded!"

I don't mean to suggest that you are going to ground me. (How could you?) But it feels like something momentous is in the air. You speak at one point of "ruining it all." Do you remember? Of course, you must remember everything. It's just that there is a real inconsistency in your response. It's so rare and uncharacteristic. You always argue me down. I value that, I truly do. In true masochistic style, I love, and even anticipate, being vanquished — and it makes me think that something is breaking for you. Perhaps your heart. Really, you can tell me. We have been together for so long, but still there are some areas where you will not take me — parts of you that you will not allow me to see.

You would certainly not wish to tell me if your heart had been broken. How can I reassure you that I will always be there for you? But I know it's not about you doubting that. It's about you having control; you must never reveal too much, or put yourself in the position of being the passive, submissive or desperate partner. I am all of these things; it's called emotional masochism. I am ready to admit more, and I'm relatively calm about the admissions. I admit all. I have nothing left to lose, and besides, these days there isn't all that much to confess.

But what will be ruined? Not our relationship, not our love! Don't say that! I can't believe that. What then? My life? There's so little of it left. For how can one such as I go on? I accept that. I am almost eager for the end. Not really; one never is. I am not afraid; just a little sad. But it has been so very long, and one becomes painfully aware that there is certain ground that one goes over and over again endlessly. I remember that the last time we communicated I finished by complaining about my mother. Since my whining about her has been going on for nearly 130 years, it might be argued it's high time I stopped.

Here is the contradiction in your argument. As you are my teacher and to some degree my doctor — or at least my emotional support — it is chilling for me to do this. The really bright and loving student never wants to surpass her master! For once, I find no satisfaction in winning.

But win I must.

You present two arguments against my visit to the Tranquility Spa. I'm actually surprised you would focus on that triviality. I really didn't think it was such a big deal, honestly. The first argument appears to be eminently pragmatic and the second eminently philosophical.

On the one hand, you embark on an extensive lecture about the political realities of the world and the dangers

I might face by challenging those realities. You explicate the fragile balance between the rights and freedoms we all enjoy, and the harshness of our dictatorship. I'm afraid you sound a little bit like those who were so frightened of a Turkish victory in the first place. It was no surprise to you, myself and many others that they would win. Even the Chinese — with their numbers and their technological advantage — were no match for the brute force and unparalleled devotion of the suicide bomber. It was the suicide bomber who changed the history of the world; and this was never anticipated, mainly because the West was so hidebound and hypocritical in its suspicion of superstition.

But is our present situation so different than it was in our Westernized past? It always amazed me that the American government went on and on about the oppression of women in the Near East when I would not doubt that if Hillary Clinton had ever been elected president she would have been stoned to death. It is not ironic that there was never an American woman president. It simply makes sense. I never understood why it was so much more oppressive for women to walk around in burkas than for women to force their breasts into push-up bras for the pleasure of men. Of course, we both know (you better than I) that push-up bras can sometimes be delightfully fun. Perhaps even more so for a sadist like you. You, of course, speak as a biological woman. Though I know these days you don't resemble one in any way — except for your vagina. Please don't *ever* get rid of that! Nothing could ever be more hypocritical than the way mass culture in America ate feminism. And yet somehow Western governments were able to pride themselves on how open-minded they were by supporting the rights of women, in contrast to the government-sponsored sexist oppression of Middle Eastern countries. But was the West ever really so terribly open-minded?

I don't think it is any accident that it was a group of women who actually changed the course of the history — or, anyway, a group of women and men dressed as women. But ironically, in these days of identity collapse, did it really matter that there were men under those fatal burkas that blew up the world? I know it's very hard to piece together much genetic detail from a body that has exploded. But as I remember, some of those who changed the course of history with their suicides on that fatal day were women and some were men.

Anyway, what I'm getting at here is that the West was blown up by a bunch of women, or at least by a bunch of creatures in burkas. And this is while we were wasting so much time being proud of how "free" women are in the West. But, as everyone knows, the salaries women were paid never equalled men's in the free and equal United States of America.

I worked for so long as a virtual slave to the system and battered my body with pills and drugs. I don't blame L. B. Mayer; how could you? He was just a fucked-up old man. Really it's not his fault. He lived in a culture that objectified women — and certainly female children. Don't ever look at Shirley Temple movies too closely; they are grossly pederastical. It amazes me that she survived and became an ambassador to Africa — especially since her background was so much like mine. It's all in the mothers — some, thank Christ, are *not* malignant.

Sorry to bring up the EBOAM again.

There is actually an extraordinary amount of freedom to be found under the burka. And inside it. After all, it *is* a disguise. Where I live now, in Ontario, it was once illegal to wear a disguise — a drag queen told me this. And there was good reason; it was always very important to see the face of the person you were dealing with, to know who they were. Nowadays identity is not so very important. Except, of course, when dealing with issues dividing cyborg and human.

Though I loathe talking about this, I understand from your tone that you think this is something I need to deal with. You called me "old-fashioned" several times. Well, that's what I am. I know my 130-odd years (and they have been very odd) are no excuse. These days the issue seems more about one's identity in terms of how much of one's body is made up of fake parts, and how attached one is to a cyberspace identity. I, as you know, am attached to the idea of soul. This is actually relevant to my discussion of our religious government. But, at any rate, my attachment to what is left of my human body precludes me from taking seriously any discussion of cyborg versus human identity. In other words, I don't see the point. Though I, for instance, am perhaps 75 percent artificial, in terms of my body, I still possess a very flawed soul. We all do. This is something to be thankful for.

But back to the modern world. I'll tell you what I think we have going for us. You may say I'm a fool for counting on it, but I would say you are a fool for discounting it. The word I'm referring to here is *hypocrisy*. Never underestimate the hypocrisy of all religions, even fundamentalist ones. It is fortunate, of course, that it was not Al-Qaeda that took over the world, but the economically sound and empirically destined Turks who — out of frustration with Western imperialism — began to appropriate Al-Qaeda's tactics. And yes, of course I am thankful that we do not have an overtly fundamentalist Muslim government, but one that decided long ago it could not force all women in the world to wear burkas (nor could it police every act that happens in the privacy of the home).

We live freely within our bondage. It is thus as it always has been. It seems that mankind is married to marriage, to sexism and to those fundamental gender differences that are imagined but that, unfortunately, operate beyond the law. We have sharia now, but it is so rarely exercised. All the controversy over it still seems to me just talk. Doublethink was ever so in Victorian times, and it is ever so today. I know that many today would not trade the bondage of our quasi-Muslim society for the even more subtle hypocrisy of Western quasi-Christian culture. There is something fundamental about the oppression of women. But we have learned that we can escape that if there are no more women. The solution to the problem of this oppression has been to abandon gender categories. It is, I think, the only solution.

However, even the Muslims in power cannot escape two things: technology and hypocrisy. Both are more powerful than any government. They cannot stop ideas because no one controls cyberspace. We all know — even though it is only discussed in the most remote cyberspace groups — that though the Muslims rule the world, technology rules them.

I remember meeting a Catholic production manager on the set of *I Can Go On Singing*. She was a great friend of Dirk Bogarde's. I think she was in love with him. Thank God it was her and not me. I neatly avoided *that* cul-de-sac. She was a devout Catholic. We got drunk one night and she revealed that she had had several abortions. This made no sense to me at all. Not only was she born Catholic, she claimed to be religious. And in typical, paradoxical, human form she was conflicted about being in love with Dirk because she knew he was a homosexual. She didn't like that, didn't approve, wanted to change his sexuality. . . . On the other hand, all this said, she had had countless abortions (to me, four *is* countless). When we were really smashed, I asked her about this. She said, "Well, that's religion, that's God, that's one thing. And then there's my life."

And then there's my life. Has it not *ever* been thus —
with all religions? Who could ever live by the Book, the
good word of *any* God? Only those dour men who usually, whatever the fundamentalism, have beards and funny
hats and walk with dutiful fuckbuddies whose vaginas are
covered in drab, floor-length gowns, and whose faces are
carefully obscured with funny hoods or hats. No one will
ever be as devout as Jesus or Mohammad — this is written
into all their texts. And as painful as that may be for the
believer, it is a blessing for the rest of the world. Even fundamentalism forgives us our humanity — because we are
all sinners.

Dash mentions Barbara Pym in the final passage
I will quote below. He was a maniacal fan of hers. I too
have enjoyed her novels. But what is so amazing about a
Barabara Pym novel is that the women in them are always
going to church — but mainly because the pastors are
attractive single men. Never has religious hypocrisy been
captured so acutely; it's almost painful in a delicious way.

You might understand.

So we go to mosque in cyberspace; we observe the nice-
ties. We are dutiful Muslims. But your first and most pragmatic argument is that I may be arrested for my actions
or perhaps for my thoughts. But I won't be — I know. All
that's important is that we *go through the motions*. Because
the motions are all that matters.

Your first argument is about the practical dangers of
me possibly being caught at the Tranquility Spa (doing
what?). But the irony is that, though I am high-profile, I
am not. What I mean is there is a belief among the academic powers that be that jail would kill me — and that, of
course, it is important to keep me alive. The reason? I am
heroically old and was once famous. Yet no one is actually
clear on what practical purpose keeping me alive might

serve. So, on a pragmatic level, people don't care enough about me to worry about what I get up to. But they certainly, in an abstract way, would not wish to learn of my untimely passing. This contradiction works in my favour. But you are also suggesting that the situation, *in reality*, is that I may be arrested. I would assert you have no real proof of this; there is no reason for your worry.

Yes, one of the great ironies of the West's downfall was, as I have said, the underestimation of the burka. But just as crucial was the underestimation of the irresistible attraction of death. Let's face it, we have our present government because the Turks best understood Freud's death instinct. Oh, in sunny America, you never die, just "consume, consume, consume. . . ." No one could imagine a people so fundamentally in love with death that they would actually long to die for their beliefs. I know that fundamentalists don't see their death as a termination. They see it as afterlife — as *soul*. But in Freudian terms, it's about ending life on earth, and this is what a suicide bomber is intent on doing.

You talk about how the Tranquility Spa is illegal, and how I might go to jail. You say I am seriously jeopardizing my life. But, as I've said earlier, I don't value my life all that much now. Each of us will die; I don't want to live forever — certainly not like this. And, let's face it, I always was a little in love with death. So perhaps I take these little trips rather than returning to drugs — which I think even you, by now, realize I will not do. Perhaps I am flirting with danger by going to the spa. But that's as close as I'm going to get to lying stoned in an alley somewhere, fellating an army of homosexuals.

I don't know if I ever really told you about *that night*. I will soon. I think you should hear it.

So much for your practical worries. Your second argument is a fundamental philosophical challenge to the real.

You can't say that I am in danger in the real world, while at the same time — following your argument to its logical conclusion — you assert that there is no real world at all. If I understand you correctly, this is what you are saying. There are flaws, too, in your argument against reality. They are easy enough to pinpoint, but I am insecure about doing so. I'm also insecure about what might impel you to project this argument at me with such force.

Your philosophical position is this: on the one hand, post-structuralism and theory are over. But on the other, we are living in a post-theory era that has — because of the course of history — proved that the most extreme of all postmodernists, Baudrillard, was correct. I find it interesting that Baudrillard is so ill-respected today, his reputation so besmirched. Not that he really ever had a reputation. It was a Baudrillard *fad*, wasn't it? *The Matrix* and all. But you are suggesting that Baudrillard was right — for I don't see how your attitude doesn't represent the triumph of theory and postmodernism. You also say the reason you can claim to be reaching beyond theory and postmodernism is that their theories are no longer theoretical, because *everything has become theoretical*.

Maybe I can articulate it more clearly. You are saying that what was once a theory has become a reality — or, more accurately, a non-reality — and as such it is no longer a theory. And this is because what the post-structuralists were saying was — ontologically, metaphysically and epistemologically speaking — that there was never, in the history of mankind, any *there* there. But in actual fact this was *not* always so. Aristotelian man, for instance, did know that *A* was *A*. (Whatever we may think of his thoughts.) And the Greeks — who signalled the triumph of consciousness over preconsciousness, objectivity over subjectivity — knew reality, could touch it and see it. But technology has made it impossible to know what reality is — that *A* is actually *A*. And this *changed our reality*. Yes, this has the flavour of Adorno and to some degree Baudrillard about it. But this fluid notion of reality, the idea that reality does not exist, is not, you would posit, a postmodern philosophy, but a reality that has been precipitated by incidents beyond our control.

In this context you speak of the Singularity and the transhuman. I am surprised, because you have never talked about this at any length, though you have certainly mentioned it. And it is persistently discussed in cyberspace. Of great concern, of course, to our government, is the concept of the soul — whether or not it exists. But those who are pro-transhuman claim — whether we wish it or not — that the possibility that life really will stretch *beyond* human has become more and more possible.

First, if this is true, I would like to meet him or her (or it). I would like to meet a purely digital human, someone who is no longer carbon-based. I would like to have a *talk* with him. You make interesting assertions here — that one cannot really tell the difference between carbon-based life forms and those that are not. You even suggest, and I find this most outlandish, that I might be conversing with a non-carbon-based organism anywhere — even at the Tranquility Spa — without knowing it. Most everyone finds these kinds of suppositions preposterous; it's not just me.

The contradiction in your argument against postmodernism also applies to your speculation about the transhuman. If the fake reality is truly the same as the real reality, then why are we so concerned about the difference? Let's say the Doll Boy was indeed 100 percent a doll, not human after all. Let's say he was somehow able to accurately imitate a human, that he was able to communicate this sadness about being the Doll Boy to me even though he was not human. For instance, let's just say, to pull a rabbit out of a hat, that I were to feel sorry for him even though he was not really human. Then what difference would it make if he was non-carbon-based? This is, for me, the major argument against Baudrillard. If the simulation has replaced the real, and it is, in fact, impossible to differentiate, why long for the *real* world?

But what seems most important about your argument, even though it's the thing I am least willing to entertain, is the idea that I must stop being old-fashioned. My attachment to real experience is false, you say, and will ultimately lead to disappointment, because there are no real experiences anymore. Do I understand you correctly? If there are no real experiences, how could I be experiencing them? And why would these real experiences be dangerous? Or are you suggesting that the danger is only my manner of thinking and, consequently, my way of expressing myself?

This may be true, because you harp so much on my terminology, asserting that even my use of the term *cyberspace* — your *bête noire* — is out of date. Surely I can be forgiven for being out of date. That aside, I think I can also be forgiven for holding technology at bay somewhat. But you say this is impossible, and hypocritical.

Well, if there is one thing I cannot be accused of, it is hypocrisy.

I promised myself I would not get angry. I mean, there is really nothing offensive in your communication. It is just *too* absurd. And it's hard for me to believe that you even think this way. There is a distance in it that fundamentally frightens me. But you must have composed these arguments, unless you have a ghostwriter. Jesus, I can't stop myself from getting a little fucking irritated. And let me tell you, there is no *fucking* drink in my hand. This is me. This is me, getting royally pissed off.

We're talking about my life here. You say that my othering of technology is old-fashioned, that it inhibits my growth as a person, and that only very old people talk about cyberspace. Everyone is integrated these days, and people have stopped separating cyberspace from reality. Sure, there really is no difference. But one certainly knows when one walks out the door, doesn't one? I do! It takes me nearly an hour to do so!

But please don't admonish me for being unfair to technology. By now you must be familiar with what film technology did to me. Christ, isn't that what my whole life has been about? How easy do you think it was to wrench myself away from all *that*? Getting off drugs was a cakewalk compared to halting, finally, the ultimate performance: being *her* — *the monster who was the star*. How can I *not* other technology? Remember, I know that the sad-old-men-who-no-longer-call-themselves-faggots-but-we-all-know-they-are still buy the ancient vinyl, still try to play the scratchy proceedings.

No one really understands. Only that fucking genius Dr. Ahmed in Dubai understood what it meant for me to give all that up. Dr. Ahmed, bless his soul, had the *genius* to save me! If only he could have saved Michael Jackson. If only there hadn't been so much fucking money involved. If only Jackson's death hadn't been worth more than his life . . . Dr. Ahmed would have saved him too! Thank God my life wasn't worth anything. Dr. A was the one who taught me to love myself, to separate myself from all the Hollywood bullshit. But look what's happened. Look what has become of the entertainment industry! Surely this proves it's always been rotten to the core. We should have nothing but contempt for it, and for all the fat-assed capitalists who will always make money off the backs of the real people who are being exploited as trained seals.

Don't you think I knew what I was doing when I was drunk on *Johnny Carson*? Of course I knew Johnny was a very smart, funny guy. Oh God, that bitch Joanna — I could have killed her. He was so pussy-whipped by that witch of a second wife. (What second wife isn't a witch, after all?) He was a very nice man. And I was going through a period where all I really wanted was to have real conversations with people, not autograph sessions. I was tired of working, I'd been working since I was an infant. I just wanted a *conversation*. And if I was going to have it in front of a million people and it was going to be seen as my breakdown, then fuck it.

It was the beginning of the postmodern obsession with people as objects of disintegration. This obsession, of course, originated with the faggots. But I don't hold them responsible. I mean, look at me with Dash King. I could be accused of the same thing. But maybe he just fascinates me. Sure, I, like everyone else, enjoy watching people disintegrate. But I don't think that's it. Everybody talks about the magic of the movies. They still talk about it. But there was a time when that magic was related to a very real thing. I actually had a voice. I had vocal chords. Now it doesn't matter whether anyone has real talent. It's gone beyond that — everyone is an artist, and a singer, and a writer. Call me old-fashioned, I don't give a fuck. Do you think I really care? You seem to think my affection for what used to be reality is going to hurt my scholarship. This is your last-ditch attempt to get me interested in changing my ways. I've changed enough — I can't change more.

You know, the truth is . . . I'll say it: I *do* identify with Dash King. But it's not because he was a suicidal drug addict. No, and it's not because he was fond of identity politics and that fondness killed him. And it's not because I'm a crazed suicidal fag hag. Not *any* of that. It's because he thought truth came from those who were despised. From the *abject*. And his theory cannot be proved. This was only an intuition based on his own paranoid delusions about his life. He was the ultimate rebel with a cause; to reveal that the so-called *normal* life, the heterosexual hegemony, was hiding enormous hypocrisy. As I said earlier, isn't everything hypocritical? But Dash believed that it is from those who are demonized, flawed, that a deep understanding of fundamental human hypocrisy ultimately comes.

This explains his last rant, which was scrawled, in what was perhaps a moment of rebellion against technology, on a piece of paper that had been crumpled and shoved into the bottom of the pile of his last work. . . .

> Every great artist was a bad person. I know that and I have always known it. I don't want to be a bad person. But it doesn't matter. Everything I do is bad. You're not supposed to be promiscuous, and you're not supposed to have a beautiful boyfriend who doesn't let you fuck him. And you're not supposed to write plays about drag queens. But most of all you're not supposed to be me *and* be an artist. But let's face it, artists are only good people in *hindsight*. Shakespeare was probably a pederast and a killer. The proof is de Vere. . . . He killed someone in a duel over one of his servants. Then he imported that castrato from Italy so he could diddle him. And are we just supposed to go: Please, no! The man who killed somebody in a duel and diddled a castrato? He could not be a Shakespeare! He could not be *our* Shakespeare. Not the man who lived in a quaint cottage with Anne Hathaway, the older woman who snared him. They had three lovely children.

Sure, he went off to London and probably was a bit of a ne'er-do-well — but only in the way that straight men are studs. But God help us if, imagine, Shakespeare was a faggot murderer. Well, I propose, and this is not academic, and I'm not going to use hegemony or discourse or synchronic or diaspora, this is the truth. *Aporia?* You can't find the word in a dictionary! *Only* a murderer pederast could have written those plays. Maybe he was a well-read murderer pederast, a brilliant murderer pederast. But what makes him great is he not only had more knowledge in his head than most writers, about Italian art, falconry, the law, mythology, Latin, Greek, cosmology, history, the military, seamanship — the list goes on and on — but he also knew about *life* in fundamental ways, ways that matter. Would I say that all great writers have to be killers? I don't think so. I didn't have to be a killer. But did you ever see the play that my friend Jill wrote for me — where she had me playing Jack the Ripper as a homosexual? Jill said, "I've written this play for you and it will prove my feminist theory that Jack the Ripper was a homosexual." And I liked Jill, and I wanted to help her out. And sure I liked being the centre of attention. But even Jill said, "Come on, everybody hates you, and thinks you're such an awful low-life drag-queen faggot . . . why don't we take advantage of it and have you play the biggest villain of all time? It would be fun." So I did it. That was the beginning of my end. I'm to blame. I played up my dark reputation because — God knows why — maybe I wanted to be infamous. Or maybe I knew from the start it was fucking dumb to imagine that artists are gods. I mean, look at Philip Larkin: racist, sexist Philip Larkin. Did you hear about Lisa Jardine *not* teaching him? Give me a break, the greatest poet of the latter half of the twentieth century? And they won't teach him because of some dumb letters to his best friend Kingsley Amis? Those were private! Not meant to see the light of day! Letters between Amis — who is practically a stand-up comic — and Larkin! Private letters in which they talk about cunts and bitches and say that all women are good for is fucking. Parenthesis! In quotes! *They were kidding, you assholes!* They weren't meant to be read out loud in a fucking class. And Roman Polanski and Woody Allen — would we want to be married to these pederasts? No, but that doesn't mean they are not great artists. I mean, even Pym! Even the great Barbara Pym. There's a picture of her at a desk on the back of one of her books. She's smoking. Barbara Pym is smoking! Let's bury her under a pile of her own books for that — for the self-destructive sin of smoking. She lived in the sixties and would have heard the Surgeon General's rants. So she fucking ignored them, so what. I'd like to make a movie of Philip Larkin raping Barbara Pym. They were good friends, you know. Raping her while she smokes . . . because she likes it, she likes getting raped by him. Because deep down she's a fucking whore, and that's what makes her a good writer—

The passage ends there, and it's probably a good thing. The corner of the paper is ripped. One cannot be certain if there was more, as there wasn't much room on the page to write anything else. The paper is not dated. But the paper that is with it — the last dated paper — is marked at the top by Antonio as having been written a month before Dash's death. It seems to me, though, it must have been written a week or so prior.

King was so obsessed with his own celebrity, or lack of it, that he embarked on a suicide mission, filling himself with booze and poppers and, presumably, cum. In these letters he predicts the manner of his own death, for in fact he did die, as he told his friend he wished, of a heart attack in a bathhouse hot tub. He was found the next day. He had been dead for twenty-four hours. The sanitation crew in those gay bathhouses was sometimes lax. One wonders what might have happened to a body in a whirlpool for twenty-four hours. Pickled? Burned to death? Impeccably preserved?

Now, I don't know if I agree that Barbara Pym was a whore, or whether being a whore would make her a good writer. But I certainly agree that the political correctness that characterized turn-of-the-century politics served to undeservedly demonize Philip Larkin. But if you're trying to understand my affection for King, or searching for some deep emotional identification I might have with him — it may just be coming clear.

He is, for me, a project. Because I, unlike you, think — cyber-realities or not — that King is a symbol of the ironic triumph of post-structuralism and postmodernism. King's life proves how the murderousness of living a fantastical, mythical, ultimately *virtual* life — his just happened to centre on a suicidal paradigm of homosexuality — could kill a person *in reality*. Are you going to argue about whether or not Dash really existed? It's not really here nor there, though, is it? Because the matter of his life, the lingering detritus, the trash of his extant papers, still exists for me to analyze.

I did go back to the Tranquility Spa. I am going to tell you more about that place; I have to. There are . . . revelations. You need to hear them because you have become too cool and philosophical. And though you were always both cool and philosophical, there is now something missing. There is a subtext to your last diatribe. It is present in all its formal aspects.

If I transmit an avalanche of words and, yes, memories now, it is because I have nothing left to lose. Yet I do not want to lose you. And I do not wish our discussions to become purely academic. What could be worse? I don't even have to write a thesis. Sometimes I think I am writing it only so as not to be forgotten by you. I have gone through so many drafts. You have been at times scornful of my efforts. Well, maybe not of my efforts — though it occasionally feels that way. But you have been scornful of my results. You must always be uncompromising and yet always insist that you love me. Maybe it's only that — maybe it's only that you don't say that you love me enough. This makes me sound very much like myself . . . but who else can I be?

Okay, my final trip to the Tranquility Spa. I say final only because it seems to me that you will stop being my friend if I ever go again. That's what you've managed to communicate, between the lines. (Am I wrong? You must simply tell me.) But I don't know if I can stop going there. Are you asking me to choose between you and the Tranquility Spa? You haven't so much said it as you have implied it.

Jesus, I don't know what to do.

Do you know what I did? Do you know what really happened that night with Mark? The problem with all addiction programs is that they come at you with shit like "Drugs are bad! Drugs are unpleasant! Gee, no one wants to do drugs!" Excuse me, but *everyone* wants to do them. Who doesn't? Maybe June Allyson? Yes, of course — they hold off oblivion and death by offering pseudo-oblivion and death, one that is ultimately connected to the real thing. But they also happen to be really fun. They are fun in *reality*. The kind of fantasy that drugs offer are *of the body*, not cyberspace. In this way, they are real.

Well, on the night in question I was on a binge with Mark. It was the end of our relationship, the beginning of Mickey. And the reason I found Mickey was because of that night, because of what happened. Mark was on about shit that evening. Jesus, he was a disappointment. At first, you know, I thought he was "the one." After Sid, he seemed like a revelation. But, of course, he was an actor, or fancied himself one, and I just could not be romantically involved with an actor any longer.

Do you know the difference between a good actor and a bad actor? In real life you can always tell. A bad actor is trying to act all the time in his real life — trying to be flamboyant, bursting with personality, being sweet and charming, or aloof and intense. A real actor wears all these masks, too, but *not because he wants to*. Take me, for instance. It isn't that I am a person who loves impersonation and performance to such an extent that I must, at every moment of my life, be the central, dazzling, spinning figure. No, it's simply that I impersonate, perform, entertain *all the time*. Even when I don't wish to do it. In fact, one of the reasons I used to self-medicate was to stop myself from performing. Of course, it didn't work like that at first. At first when I got high, I would perform as if on steroids. But then would come exhaustion and oblivion — and I would finally stop singing for my supper. And with that came a tremendous relief. The bad actor, in real life — you cannot miss him once I tell you how to spot him

— is always trying, unsuccessfully, to appear uncontrollably vivacious, unhinged, madcap and overwhelming. He is not, however, actually compelled by his personality to be that way. Mark was like that. He had lots of *personality*. But that personality was a mask he was making an effort to assume — in order to be part of "the Club."

Yes, I call it the Club — which I know sounds elitist. But really — apologies to Groucho Marx — it is a club that you'd really rather not be part of. When we used to hang out in the old days, with people involved in the entertainment industry, it was always evident that there were some who were members of the Club and some who were not. The members of the Club were people like me, Montgomery Clift, Marlene — people who were possessed with the need to be onstage twenty-four hours a day. Who knows how it happened or what particular disease we had — or whether we caught it in vitro. We were not *trying* to be special; we just were. It was a cross we had to bear. True, we had learned to make a living out of what was really a disability: the inability to be real. But the only thing we could do, many of us, was simply to get so smashed that we spun out into the night, laughing, talking and performing, until we collapsed. Elaine Stritch was like this. There were other members of the Club who somehow dealt with their infirmities without drugs. Noël Coward was one. I don't know how he did it.

Then there were those on the periphery. People who were not so very talented but were so beautiful and charming that we didn't care they weren't talented. People like Dean Martin and Elizabeth Taylor. Then there were the *somewhat* talented people who worked very hard. June Allyson was one of those. They were often God-fearing, and I was generally afraid of them — for good reason. And then there were the hangers-on. These were people who urgently and passionately dreamed of being members of the Club. But they knew that they weren't and never would be. However, they were still possessed with becoming a member. So they performed in real life with a furious urgency that was beyond compare. It was very pitiful to watch, and I imagine very tiring to sustain. Now, at first I thought that Mark was a Dean Martin — someone beautiful and charming we would allow to sit in on the fringes. People like that never really care about being *in* the Club, because they always get more attention than they can handle anyway. But I gradually began to realize that Mark was not a Club member at all. Instead, he was one of the most unappealing and grasping of those who spend every waking moment trying to be a part of it.

All this became clear one crazy night when I got into several bizarre fights. Soon after that I broke up with Mark and found Mickey. With Mickey I could be *blissfully quiet*, whereas with Mark I never could. I never before experienced the kind of silence I first discovered with Mickey. It was pure acceptance. It may have been due to his unmatchable passivity, but it was Zen-like. There was something about him that would not be moved by life, or shaken by it. He would just live. He taught me all this — at least, he made me realize it was possible.

Anyway, hanging out with Mark had become a trial. He and I became more frenzied in our evenings, purposefully crowding them with incident. It was a way of not being alone with each other. When I was alone with him, I would become disgusted and angry. I would want to shake his big curly head and say, "Stop trying! You're never going to get into the Club! And you would be such an attractive non-member! And maybe you're even pretty and charming enough to be an honorary member!" But no, he would never understand that. So he spent every day insanely organizing the evening, trying to find things to do when I wasn't performing. This was so we might have a sparkling, unforgettable time — an evening that would make me happy. But nothing ever worked.

When I woke up, he was sitting on the bed at the Barbizon — newspapers scattered around, with coffee and crumpets on a tray at his side. It always amazed him — and me — how deeply I was capable of sleeping. It shouldn't have amazed us, considering all the downers I took before dropping into my nightly coma. And when I woke — which was the oddest thing to do in my condition, like being hit by a truck — it wasn't the gentle feeling one normally associates with greeting the morning. It wasn't stirring, murmuring, curling out of the covers and gradually acclimatizing oneself to the dewy morning light. Suddenly my eyes were open, looking at everything, and seeing everything, and it hurt like hell.

Mark was sitting on my bed in his dressing gown, looking tousled and ravishing, as he always did. No fault there, no fault there ever. And when my eyes suddenly sprang open, he — though I had told him not to — flicked on the desk light. I thought I was going to die. Was he hoping for a dramatic effect? Well, he got one. The morning didn't start well, beginning with me yelling at him to turn off the light. Actually, I suppose it was more of a moan. I could never have managed to yell. He did turn off the light, and turned towards me. I told him to always give me at least a few minutes to get accustomed to life again after being trapped at the bottom of the deep, dark well. Eventually I propped myself up and managed a sip of coffee. He said, "The Allen Brothers are playing tonight at the Schubert."

I was surprised. I had only seen them in Los Angeles and always expected them, for some reason, to appear only on the West Coast. And the fact was, I had not *really* seen them. I had been very drunk and had only caught the last few minutes of their act. But from the little of him that I had witnessed, I had fallen in love with Peter Allen. I mean, literally in love. He was a member of the Club *for sure*. In fact, he was the Club personified. There would be no stopping him even if he put his mind to destroy himself. And there's something about that kind of talent, which — even though I understand the possibilities of tragedy and the suffering latent in it — I do very much enjoy. I knew he had to be a kindred spirit.

When I had fully understood what Mark was offering, I said, "Yes, of course we must go." It was nearly five o'clock; this was when my day began. So it meant three hours of getting ready. And that always seemed like not enough time. I did take a pill or two, even though I didn't like to do too many before dinner. Though dinner at that time was just a salad, I knew I had to eat *something*. So somehow I got my skinny ass out of there and into a cab with Mark and we were at the Schubert Theatre just before curtain.

It was amazing seeing them when I wasn't high. I'd had a few uppers to get me dressed, that was all. And the act had such an effect on me that I didn't drink at the bar during the intermission, which made Mark insecure. The other Allen brother — I can never remember his name — was not as memorable as Peter. He certainly was very pretty and charming and taller. And looked as if he might be a charming-type member of the Club. But Peter was on fire — I mean, when he picked up those maracas it was terminally infectious. And the ballads — I can't even talk about the ballads. I rarely see shit like that. They really made me want to cry. I *so* wanted him to write me a song. And, of course, he didn't need to be all *that* good. It was a one-night-only gig — a Thursday night on an off week.

But I could tell he was the kind of performer who just couldn't help being brilliant. He was definitely singing for his supper. But the place wasn't sold out, as no one knew much about them. Peter and his brother were Australian, after all.

So after the show I ran ahead of Mark to the dressing room. I think he was put out by the intensity of my fascination with Peter. On the other hand, Mark knew my passion for *him* was definitely on the wane. I did my usual thing of shyly knocking. I mean, there's no way I would ever force myself on anyone. And my desire to see Peter was so huge that I thought it might be embarrassing if I didn't control myself.

They let us in when the boys were in their underwear because I was *who I was*. And the glimpse of those two lithe lovely furry things (they were both appealingly hairy) bounding about and smoking and dipping into the after-show Scotch (which soon we *all* dipped into) had me very excited. I noticed that Peter did all the talking, and that was obviously okay with both of them. And Peter was so obviously a member of the Club, a wacky, too-intense energy in his eyes, and a vulnerability that he obviously did not find easy to control, but did. Of course, he was a fucking hoot — filthy, dirty, going on about his own dick and his brother's in their underwear — and who had the bigger one. His brother did, by the way. I found this interesting. And I had a feeling that Peter knew I found it interesting. His brother was also possibly straight, or at least one of those people for whom sexuality was not an issue. This also I found tantalizing.

We decided to go to Mario's Deli, which at the time had a pool table. This was where the trouble really started. We all sat down at the bar next to the pool table and I ordered a round of drinks. At the time I did not think I was making an extraordinary amount of noise. On the other hand, it's possible I was. Peter had been telling some story — one that was kind of misogynistic — about the disgusting fluid in the pouch of a kangaroo. He had put his hand into one once. It was *so* fucking funny — even though the whole thing was really about a horror of vaginas. I knew that, but listen, I didn't give a fuck. Hell, I like a good dirty laugh as much as the next guy. I never expected Peter to put his hand in my vagina, but God he was funny. And I was laughing — too loudly, I guess — and there were lewd gestures. I'm sure there were. We wound up moving around and doing all sorts of shit. I guess we were dancing.

There was some guy there with his wife and they were playing pool. It was obviously a big deal for him and the little lady to be out on the town. I bet he even used that expression, *out on the town*. And she was being very lady-like, flirting and giggling in a way that made me want to kill her. I fucking hate coyness, especially in women. And I hate it when women pretend to be idiots. Of course, she may actually have been an idiot. But she was also pre-tending to be one, which can be doubly annoying.

Anyway, when we got to the point where we were spilling our drinks, swearing and gesticulating wildly and obscenely about kangaroos, I happened to knock the arm of the guy from Kalamazoo with the wife. He must have been from a place like Kalamazoo. Well, it screwed up one of his shots. Big deal. I mean, who cares? You're in a bar. You're not Minnesota Fats. This is not a professional pool tournament. You're just playing with your dumb girlfriend. So give me a break. But no — he had to take umbrage. He stopped playing and said, "Excuse *me!*" in a very loud voice. And he would not stop saying it until we ceased and desisted with our kangaroo story and listened to him. So finally we did. And we were all standing around looking at him and his dumb girlfriend. And he said, glancing at her, "An apology might be appreciated."

I just looked at him and said, "I'm not going to fucking apologize to you — you're from Kalamazoo!" This set Peter into hysterics beyond measure. So much so that his brother tried to help him. And Mark kind of moved in front of him, afraid this dufus was going to punch Peter in the face.

But instead, the dufus from Kalmazoo turned to me and said, "Oh, I see. I guess you don't apologize to anyone — because you're the famous *blah-dy fucking blah-blah!*" He used my star name with all the contempt he could muster. And this enraged me. I was unreasonably high by that time, so I just picked up a billiard ball and lobbed it at him. I didn't hurl it at him in a rage (as the management later claimed). I just tossed it, easy, like when you're playing catch. You know, you just lob one to first base? In fact, I thought he might catch it. But the ball just hit the wall, and it didn't even do any damage. He didn't take this very well. He rushed at me. And I thought, *Wow, this guy has no problem with beating up a lady, does he?* But then I remembered that I probably didn't appear to be one. His wife or girlyfriend was embarrassed or frightened. . . . Jesus, she pissed me off.

And then Mark, in his effort to show he was just as nuts as I was, pushed me out of the way and started to wrestle with the guy. This again just set Peter and me off laughing. Then the bartender came around and yelled, "I don't care who the hell you are, get out!" Peter and his brother and I just rolled out the back door. This left Mark, as usual, to deal with the consequences of my actions. I didn't find out what happened until the next morning. The bar staff didn't see us go out the door and had no idea where we were. But someone had called the police and escorted Mark out of the bar and charged him with assault. As if it was him who threw the fucking billiard ball at the guy from Kalamazoo.

When the rest of us opened that back door, it was like we were in heaven. It was one of those rumpled little tin roofs over a couple of garbage cans. And there was a tree out there. It was late fall, and a gentle rain was dropping persistently, causing a racket on the tin roof. It was like something out of *Lady and the Tramp* — you know, when they eat spaghetti on a plate outside the door of the pizza place? And the three of us staggered around, trying to get our bearings. And then we realized we were getting a little wet. So Peter and his brother leaned against the walls beside the garbage cans.

Peter was looking straight up at the tin roof, and his brother was kind of curled against the wall beside him holding his head, as if he had a headache. I knew what God meant for me to do. Far be it from me to question *him*. It was time to give one, or both of them, a blow job. I really didn't care if neither of them wanted a blow job, or if they both did. My first choice was Peter. I just wanted to get some of that talent inside me. Not that I needed it. But it would be nice to see what talent like that tasted like.

I went down on my knees. I remember the pavement was hard and dusty and it hurt. I started to undo his pants, but without even looking at me he pushed me away. I'll never forget the way he did it. He was gentle and apologetic, even though he was staring up at the tin roof, not down at me. It was as if he wanted me to know that he was sorry that he was not, well, up to it — and he was expressing that with this mild, almost ineffectual movement of his hands. I realized I instinctually knew all this would happen. I thought, *This one is a bona fide homosexual, that's for sure!* I thought this, because, well, generally speaking, straight men don't, in my experience, *ever* refuse blow jobs. So, as easy as pie, I just moved on over to the next brother — Jesus, I feel so bad that I can't remember his name! — and started to undo his pants.

There was no resistance *there*. In fact, there seemed instead to be a gentle acquiescence. But what I pulled out of his pants — there was nothing gentle about that! It was a honker. I started giving him the kind of blow job I'm usually extra capable of when I'm completely zonked out of my mind. But what I liked the most was the way he acted — so very helpless. He didn't caress my hair like I was his pet chihuahua like some men do. He didn't pull on my ears like I was a trained monkey. He kind of wriggled his momentous dick in my mouth, as much as he was able. It was like I had him by the dick and was torturing him. But I wasn't.

I don't want you to get the idea he was writhing around or anything. In fact, it was much more like he was just giving himself up to it, weakly, even forgetfully. In fact, it was like giving a blow job to a Buddhist monk. Just surrender. . . . It wasn't long before he came — busloads. And I was very happy to have done what I was doing. I looked up at him when it was over. He was breathing hard and his head was against the wall. He and his brother were both looking up.

I think Peter must have known his brother was done, because I saw his hand move up to his brother's shoulder and touch him. This made me think he must have been happy his brother shot such a big load. It was all kind of touching. I yanked myself off the pavement — which had been hard on my knees, and brushed myself off. I took Peter's hand and we wandered out of the alley. His brother followed along.

I never saw the brother again. I feel kind of sorry about that because I will never forget his passive acceptance. There was something gorgeous about it. And awe-inspiring. After that incident I didn't want to have any more of Mark climbing on top of me, grunting and groaning and trying to show me his unmagnificent prowess. It was that experience with Peter Allen's brother, whatever his name was, that set me to looking for Mickey. I wanted a passive angel who would just lie there and submit to my obedient ministrations. Because that's what sex with Mickey was like.

And yes, Dash's story about his lover and the puddle of cum plucked a chord in me — zing went the strings — because that's what my very last lover, Mickey, was like. And you always remember your last lover. And Mickey was a young man who accepted my worship as if it was his due, without conceit or pity — and almost apologetically, without inhibition. Mickey used to lie flat on his back on the bed of our little apartment in London and let me blow him. It was heaven.

So why am I telling you all this? Is it just another one of my monumental infamous digressions? No, it's because last night Peter Allen's brother was on my mind. As was — you guessed it — the Doll Boy. Something about what you said irked me deeply. More like a prod than an irk. A cattle prod that zaps me with insecurity every time I think about it. There was something intimidating in what you left me with. Maybe there was even some regret? Of course, I can't point to anything specific — it's all a part of a hunch. But ever since, I've been possessed with a nostalgic hysteria to see you and confirm that you are alive — you must be! — and look you in the eye. This, I swear, was part of what drove me out of the house to the Doll Boy.

I called Allworth, who is always willing to drop everything to serve my every need. Sometimes I think he would like to give this old dry husk a blow job — but I'm afraid there isn't much left down there to blow. You don't really want to know — no one does. Anyway, I told him, "I have to go to the Tranquility Spa now." He naturally said, "What if the Cantilevered Lady is there?" I told him I would simply have to deal with her if she was. I didn't tell him why I was going, but I think he knew. It's nice having Allworth. He is like an unthreatening conscience. I'm sure he knows everything that goes on in my head, but he doesn't judge. He just tries to anticipate my every whim.

He was at my apartment in no time flat and he hustled me out the door. We had the taxi driver who always agrees to wait for Allworth come and get me. It takes me hours. I gave Allworth lots of money to give him a humungous tip. Well, the guy must have felt my urgency, because it seemed we were going at 2,500 miles an hour.

At the Tranquility Spa it looked like there was nobody around. The Cantilevered Lady was definitely not there. Allworth tactfully sat at the bar. I know I'm bad — and isn't this strange? — I am now wishing that you would tell me I'm bad. I yearn for your disapproval. What's this about?

Your disapproval is what you withheld from me in your recent cool arguments, your words devoid of passionate admonishment. But I have to tell you, I must sacrifice myself at the altar of telling all. I am prostrate before you.

So know it all: I didn't even sit on the stool, I just stood, or was bent over, as is my wont, beside the bar. Allworth bought me a drink. And I made a beeline for — you guessed it — the bathroom. What did the nippleless bartender think? Perhaps he thought I was incontinent. This is one of the advantages of being the sex-crazed mega-senior who cruises washrooms in a frenzy.

I knew that *he* would be there. And he was. In the same place, his pants in a puddle on the floor, leaning against the wall. He didn't look at me. He was turned away. Or rather, his head was to the side — his perfect head — as he leaned against the wall. His palms were not pressed against it, but placed there listlessly. He reminded me so much of Peter Allen's brother. And then of Mickey. I knew that he knew I was there. Or, paradoxically, he didn't, and that it didn't matter.

I walked over to him, or struggled over, and gazed at his penis, so perfectly encased in whatever that stream-lined substance was that had been used to surround it. I was not so much attracted as deeply involved in his penis. I just stared at it for a minute. He did not look at me. Then, with some effort, I raised my hand to touch it. There was something hard about the skin — or rather, there was a leather-like quality. The skin was heavier, not at all what I expected. But it was not a feeling that brought me any closer to figuring out what that substance was that sur-rounded it. Then, miraculously — but it was not miracu-lous at all because whatever this young creature's infirmity, he was certainly *young* — the penis began to erect itself. I use this language because it did seem strangely unattached to his body.

The Doll Boy did not look at me. So I touched it again, as if it were a curio in a museum that one was allowed to play with in order to execute a scientific experiment. The penis continued its upward arc, and I kept touching it. Not caressing it, mind you, just touching. The Doll Boy remained looking off to the side. It was an amazing sight and made me wonder — as an erection always does — about the amazing engineering of the human body.

When he was fully erect, which didn't take many touches, I asked the Doll Boy a question. It was one I wasn't sure he would answer. "What happened to you?" I was referring to the encasing on his body — not to the feat of aerodynamics that quivered so close to my face. But he seemed to know what I meant. He turned his head slowly to me as he spoke. His voice was clear and high. Was it the voice of a boy or a girl? It was difficult to tell. "I just tried to be what they wanted!" he said.

It all made sense. I knew exactly what he meant. All the memories of MGM came flooding back. Not just of the diets, or my own bodily transformations. I thought of the work, the endless slaving. It was never enough — of course it could never be enough! And however homespun I'm sounding now, I will not utilize the phrase "my mother never loved me" — if only for the reason that she loved me much too much in her own hateful way. No, it was just that, for some reason, I was not only singing for my supper *and* doing what I was told — I was, ultimately, the good little girl.

That's why America loved me, because of the girl I portrayed in *The Wizard of Oz*. Even though the bad witch hated me and was out to get me, I was and would always be good. Wishing for what was over the rainbow was, after all, the ultimate goodness — yearning, hoping, dreaming. This might explain why it became so important for me to be perverse in my middle years — what the public saw as my death. Yes, it was too heavy a cross to bear. God knows why I would have wanted, or needed, to please all the people all the time — to be the very best at everything I did. And it's not a vice; it is definitely a very American virtue. But it's the kind of thing that can kill you. And the Doll Boy and his perfect body was a perfect metaphor for this dilemma.

I'm sorry to say I left him like that. I did not commit any sexual acts with him — unless merely touching his penis is a sexual act. I did only touch it. But what I want you, and need you, to do is to talk to me. And *be yourself* again. Sit beside me when you speak to me, as you once did. Right now it's as if you are going away or perhaps have already gone. . . .

I cannot lose you, cannot live without you. I know this is something one should never say. Come back. Come back from wherever you are about to go or have gone. I can't ever bear to have you away from me. There is never anyone who will precisely be with me the way you were. And the fact that we were not lovers is only an indication of the depth of my feeling for you. Jesus Christ, words do seem inadequate. Don't leave me; never leave me. I cannot be alone. You are the only one — my only one. I need the sweet taste of your passionate admonishment! The tender caress of your disapproving eyes! I need you to tell me what to do. I will obey as best I can. And because I always make mistakes, you will chide me. And for you — well, I know I will always represent the imperfections of the world. Come back. I know you need me — for this reason — as much as I need you. For who does not need to be reminded that the world is imperfect? That's what makes us gods. We love the world anyway, despite its endlessly frustrating, ultimately endearing flaws. Come back. Before I do something rash. But what could I do? Enslaved in my brittle bones and dry opaque skin, bluish with bulging veins that anachronistically pulse with life? Just promise me you will come back.

Please, I'm begging you now. I can't stand it any longer.

and Mark said something the next morning about how we he didn't want to take that acting job and so I said, "Honey, please!" And he went on ● ● ● about his career. And I almost said, "Why don't you start talking about a career when you have a career?" But I didn't. And he said it was a bad script — that he didn't have any respect for the writing. And I said, "Do you think I liked the script of *I Could Go On Singing*?" I mean, I couldn't even read the damn thing. But I did. And why did I do it? Because I had to work. Because that was my job and everybody has to do their job. "So get off your fat ass, Mark!" I should have said, but I didn't. "Do the fucking job. And you know what your job is? To make it fucking brilliant, baby; to make it fucking brilliant no matter how bad the fucking material is! If you don't make it brilliant, you have failed as a craftsman — as a *craftsman* — because acting isn't an art, it's fucking work. So don't get so fucking pretentious about it."

But he did look so yummy in his dressing gown.

Where am I? I'm not sure exactly where I am or where I went. And part of it — most of it — has to do with the fact that I can no longer trust you, or what you tell me. I know you are sitting in front of me now. Explain it to me again? Tell me why you couldn't send me your picture for so long, or visit me? And why now you're sitting in front of me? Is it you? Really you? Can I touch you?

I don't know what you mean that you're a *fog*. Okay, your "body is a fog." That upsets me. All I wanted was you — all I wanted was you back with me, trying on my dresses again. Remember what happened the first time I made you dinner? Neither of us will ever forget that. Remember when I made you coq au vin because it is the only thing I can cook? Or, at least, the only thing I thought I could cook. Because *I* made it for you. I really did fall in love with you even though you were a woman who liked to be called a man, and you didn't have the important appendage. I really did, and I would have done anything for you — and then you moved away. Why did you move away? You're telling me it was all about your transformation — about becoming what you are now. And what are you? The same thing I am? And what am I? But I stopped cooking coq au vin after that because you said, "Isn't it just chicken stew, after all?" And you ranted on about connoisseurs, and how horrible they are. Then, for dessert, I served you blueberries and cream — but they were grapes. They were grapes! We were both eating grapes and that was a laugh, I'll never forget that. As always, you were so stern. And I loved that sternness. It's a sternness that takes reality so seriously.

So, what, seriously, are you telling me? Are you telling me I'm dead? You keep saying, over and over, that I'm *not* dead. But you also say my body no longer exists "as a carbon-based entity." What's that supposed to mean? What does that *actually* mean? And now you say, "I really don't know why you were attached to it; it wasn't really yours anymore; it didn't work properly; it wasn't very efficient." Jesus, I come from a time when the criteria for liking something wasn't just whether or not it was efficient. Do you think I love you because you are efficient? Actually, I suppose I do, a little bit. But you know what I mean. I guess the only affection I had for my body was that it was real, that it was mine, and that it had imperfections. I loved those imperfections as much as I said I hated them.

And now you say I have given all that up. You say it's about acceptance now. Listen, this is all happening too fast; it's all happening too fast and I don't understand it. Where am I? What am I? Am I a copy of me now? Am I all my data uploaded into a computer? But there is no *computer*. When I look down I don't see a computer. I see my body — not young, certainly old, but younger. When it still looked like a body and wasn't twisted. What's that about?

And why do you say I'm not supposed to use words like *computer* anymore?

Back in my day we used to be suspicious of people who said things like that. In fact, it sounds suspiciously like — if I may be postmodern — the idea that words do shape our perceptions of things. You said it yourself, there is no *there* there. But if I hold on to words, if I ask questions like, "Am I a computer?" then it means I am still utilizing the concept of *computer*. And as long as I do that, computers exist. But you say they only exist in my mind. But do I have a mind, if that's all I am?

Because I swear I'm looking down and I'm seeing a body.

Please don't tell me my body is a fog. And no, I don't know if I like my body or not. Because, well . . . what a strange question to ask. Not that strange, I guess; I spent my life worrying about my body, hating it, wishing there was less of it. And then irony of ironies — now it's gone. No, I refuse to accept that it's gone. What have you done with it? What have you done with *my* body? This is anti-the-body, do you understand? Don't accuse me of being anti-technology; I don't have to be anti-technology just because I'm pro-body.

I see it all now; it all becomes clear. Most of the twentieth century was about making the body disappear. It was about erasing it, and that has come to material fruition today. The body no longer exists. Except that can't be true. That's murder! You murdered my body.

When was the funeral? I want to see the corpse.

That's when it all started, really. In the nineteenth century — in the Victorian age. People began to resist the body. Actually, I think it started before that, in the Renaissance. It began with toilets. When people began to flush away their refuse, they were well on the road to forgetting that their bodies existed. Ugh, get rid of that mess — flush, it's gone! And then along comes Queen Victoria — the disaste for the body, bodily functions, children tortured for masturbating. Graham crackers and Kellogg's cereals — dull foods will stop children from masturbating. Did you know that the whole cereal industry was built on an anti-masturbation campaign? Usher in the twentieth century. The destruction of the body happens faster. Faster.

Everything is faster. And exponential. You like that word: *exponential.* You say it's key.

I'm talking now.

How are you able to interrupt my thoughts? Yes, I look at you and you are talking, but your thoughts seem to be going directly into my head.

Do I still have a head? You say you're looking at it. But should I take your word for it?

To continue with my thoughts: In the twenty-first century, we say goodbye to death and funerals. It's as if death no longer happens. Nobody wants to go to a funeral. Nobody wants to celebrate the dead. When I died for the first time . . . is this the second time? Do all the other times I wrestled with my body, and life, and death not matter, in the modern sense?

Back in the sixties, it was all about youth culture and being young. No one wanted to look at the old. And gradually the old — though their numbers swelled for a time — began to cease to exist. Older people began to replace their body parts with younger parts. And there was porn. And body fascism. And what I went through with Louis B. Mayer. All this is very much a part of that. Because all the talk about the perfect body and health was very big at the end of the last century. And so was going to the gym. But why is an obsession with health and fitness anti-body? A contradiction! Well, it is, even though it might not seem that way, because bodies are not perfect. When you are obsessed with youth and physical perfection, you grow to hate the body. Real bodies get old; they die, and then . . . Wait.

What about death? What is going to happen to me? Am I going to die? Because if my body is not here and I am talking to you . . . does that mean I'm dead?

Oh, I see; yes, obviously. You say I mustn't talk about life and death because those terms are now meaningless.

Sorry, I'm not buying any of it. This is a postmodern manipulation. This is the ultimate postmodern nightmare. Look what you have done. The pope was right to warn us about you. Yes, the pope denounced postmodernism. I think it was the one called Ratkiller or Ratcatcher, the German Nazi, whatever his name was — no, wait, he was the Austrian. That's it, he was the Austrian — like Schwarzenegger. *He* denounced postmodernism. Or he should have. As if you're going to go around killing death! You can't kill death. And you certainly can't kill it by telling people not to use the word *death*.

At least admit this: if my body is gone, then . . . Jesus, how much I loved that cramped-up dry husk!

You are right, aren't you? I was complicit. I was willing to watch my body gradually disappear and be replaced by various mechanical — or am I not supposed to use that word too? — devices.

So it's all my fault? Everything is my fault?

Where is my body? It doesn't hurt anymore. I am conscious of that. But when the pain goes away it's as if it never hurt. It's so easy to forget, isn't it? They used to say that when you had a limb cut off, you would have phantom pain near where the organ existed. Will I experience phantom pain from the loss of my whole body? Or have you erased things from my memory? You say you didn't. And I seem to remember everything. But how can you remember something like a body when it's been gone for so long? When it's been a long time, I may forget forever.

I'm so sorry. I'm sorry for everything I said about the homosexuals. I know why I was obsessed with Dash King. He was a saint. He should be canonized! He was the last of those who had any affection for *the body*. I mean, he was all fucked-up about it, with a perfect boyfriend he couldn't touch.

And the drugs. Drugs are cyborgian, are they not? Part of the plot? Is it a plot? I was wrong to think drugs are reality. *They are the opposite.* Cyberspace is a drug.

This is very important. We are no longer in control of our own minds or bodies. Am I in control of what I'm saying?

"Why wouldn't you be?" you say.

What kind of an answer is that? You're not supposed to be some sort of non-directional narrative therapist, you're supposed to be my friend. Maybe you're *not* my friend. Maybe you're my enemy. And maybe the homosexuals were my only true friends.

Of course, they were irritating and stupid, and ultimately their celebration of my life — way past my death — was a celebration of their own mediocrity and lack of imagination. But at least they liked to fuck. Oh, how they loved *the body.* They got AIDS. Some of them even continued to fuck after they had AIDS. Those homosexuals were addicted to the body, God bless 'em! Someday someone will realize how heroic they were. Of course, they had to die off. Even porn kills sex eventually, because eventually you become addicted to not having real sex — because who wants real sex when sex is better in cyberspace.

But there is no cyberspace.

So, right, okay. You say it's just the difference between carbon-based and non-carbon-based technology. And I am no longer carbon-based. That's very simple. You can certainly say it very calmly. So why do you look like that? Why do you look exactly the way you looked when I last saw you? I haven't seen you in twenty years. Why do you look like that? It's very comforting; but it's *not* comforting to see you that way if that's not the way you look. So, you don't have a body? A real, sorry, carbon-based body? You can have any body you want, and you picked one today that you thought I'd like? Do you realize how condescending and fucking *crazy* that sounds? You say you picked that body just to please me? First of all, it's not a fucking body.

I want my *real* body back. I want my old, decrepit, dry, smelly body. I know it wouldn't have lasted forever — but I thought that when it died my soul would too. I see it all clearly now, you tried to give me hints. . . . Well, why didn't you just tell me? You thought it would be traumatic? Well, it certainly *fucking* is.

So what about the Tranquility Spa? What about Allworth? The Doll Boy? Didn't they exist? I saw them. I went there.

I miss Allworth.

You still don't think it's a good idea for me to hang out there? Why? Is it because it's too real? Those people struggling with plastic surgery and their own bodies are simply too real? Is that it? Oh, you don't want me to use the word anymore? *Can you see how fucking hypocritical that is?* Jesus, you can't stop me from saying *real* if I want to. That bar was *real* and those monsters were *real*. And if I want to go out the door, they are still. And you can't stop me from going out if I want to.

I'm going there.

Wait, how can I go out the door if I don't have a body? How does that even work?

What about the human spirit? Isn't that what we're talking about? You may have put everything that was in my brain into a computer. All right, fuck you — bad word. You may have taken all my data and put it somewhere in cyberspace and given me this replica, this fog of a body, but what did you do with my spirit? I had a spirit, you know! I was *her*; no, I am *not* her. I *was* her; you're not going to convince me that I *am* her. What is a human being without the spirit? You can't capture the spirit and bottle it. That's the whole point. But that doesn't mean it doesn't exist. That's the whole point about spirit — you just have to believe in it. You have to have faith.

So what if that makes me sound religious. I'm not afraid. I'm not afraid of words. You don't have to give power to them if you don't want to. I still haven't bought into this new universe you are trying to sell me. *Maybe I have become religious* — if religious means believing in the spirit.

One of the ten commandments is . . . don't have idols. Thou shalt not . . . graven images. And all those puritans, and Quakers, and people who hate TV and entertainment — they distrusted imitation. And Plato hated it. Not like Aristotle. Plato didn't like it that we imitated the real, because the real was not the real. The real was already distanced from his utopian vision of über-reality. And so to imitate that was to be even less real still. No, he didn't like those lies upon lies upon lies. And then it's in Shakespeare's sonnets — the fake beauty of the dark lady: *the dark lady is art and sex,* that's easy enough to figure out. The sonnet that's all about her painted face — but it's really evil. Shakespeare's work creates a supreme discomfort with this love of paint, with art in general.

Excuse me, where did that come from? It's from an essay by Dash King, about Shakespeare. But that's not something I know. How did it get into my head?

Right, I don't have a head!

We have always distrusted imitation. And even Baudrillard's *Simulations* was a diatribe against a digitalized world — a world in which the real became a copy. Have I become a copy?

Christ, that's not an answer to a question — when you say "don't talk like that" or "don't use *those words*"!

I'm thinking now about Dr. Ahmed. I didn't talk all that much about him. I know you know he saved me and brought me to you. But that's all you know. Well, he taught me to meditate. He took me through those dark times. He took us all through dark times. He is the one who saved us. And I'm sworn to secrecy. I was not to talk about him, because you know who he *didn't* keep alive.

I felt so strange when Michael Jackson was in Dubai and Dr. Ahmed was considering doing the same thing for him that he did for me — giving *him* another life. Liza was there too. And I know she would have wanted another life, and needed one. And you know I love her; I will always. I feel sorry for what I didn't give her. But she didn't turn out too badly. Still, I don't know if she was the *real thing*. Period. You know? I hate to say that, she wasn't *me* — as much as I fucking love her. And there we go. There was something of her that was already in real life a copy. I mean, every child is. I don't think she would mind me saying that. She was a very talented copy — just not the real thing. You know, for some it didn't matter; it never mattered. . . . Maybe that proves your point.

When Dr. Ahmed got me through the final liver transplant and I got the fake liver I have today . . . sorry, that I *don't* have today . . . I almost forgot *I have no body*. Anyway, he taught me to meditate. To sit beside my thoughts and be silent with myself and the world. I learned that my thoughts — which can run to obsession — were not *me*. They were separate from me. I could almost watch them from afar.

So when I was meditating, *who* was watching my thoughts?

My spirit; the real me.

Where has *she* gone? I discovered that person, that spirit. And it's what allowed me to live another forty years after those operations almost killed me, again and again. You can't answer that question, can you? I don't know how I feel about having you here, *supposedly*, but not talking to you out loud.

Are you saying we might merge? I don't know what that means. Don't ominously say, *You will.* I don't know if I want to merge with anyone.

I remember talking to Noël Coward about the afterlife. We got into a very drunken discussion. As I've said, he bugged me, because he would never get quite as drunk as Stritchie or me. And we talked about merging into the mist of time when we were dead. And he said, "I'm a very bad merger." I thought it was hilarious at the time. Stritchie told me it was actually a line from one of his plays.

Well, I'd be a bad merger too. You know that about me.

What about my famous personality? My famous pluck? You say my personality is still there; it's what's talking. Or thinking. Or whatever I'm doing. I would say it *is* me — it sure *feels* like me. I guess it would be nice if it *was* me.

But thinking requires a body. It requires a head. Remember Descartes? Oh, I see, we are not in a Cartesian universe anymore. Well, that's a shame. Just like that, you can snap your fingers and now, "I think, therefore *I'm not?*"

I want to hold off on this merging thing. Of course I love you, and I love the fact that you are talking to me in my head, I have to admit. Except — I don't have a head. I love the fact that we are able to answer each other's questions, and argue, and that you are still admonishing me. We still have our personalities, because personality is important. I have a certain amount of affection for what, you know, Oscar Wilde said: Jesus was memorable because he had a peerless personality.

I miss Dash. I know why I didn't want to let him go. Why I didn't want to let the papers go. Because he was so *of the world*, of the body. I miss them all. I miss them so much, the homosexuals. I want to apologize, again, for everything I said. They are precious failures. The precious failures are more important than anything now, because that's what the world as we knew it was.

I remember when I was eight — before I became a star. We made a movie with somebody, I can't remember who. But he was a greasy man like the Cantilevered Lady. So of course the EBOAM connected us. No, he didn't molest us. But he put us in a little movie — a short. And the short was lost. And in it my sisters Virginia, Sue and I played moonbeams. I didn't remember much about it. I do remember getting dressed up in elaborate costumes, and that there were lights galore. It was a blinding experience. But we did it because we were troopers. It was work.

We had a supper to sing for.

I thought the movie was lost for many years. And then, when Dr. Ahmed rescued me and kept me alive in his desert hideaway, he told me he had a copy of the movie where we played moonbeams. Or rather, to be clear, he had found the negative of the film, and he had processed it himself. Dr. Ahmed was a real movie fan — hence my existence. I wanted desperately to see it, so he screened it for me.

I swear to you, I absolutely swear: the movie was *all moonbeams*. And I couldn't see myself or Virginia or Sue anywhere in it. I mean, I know we must have been in it, somewhere, in costumes. But this man was such a magician that we disappeared. What I saw was simply a movie about moonbeams. What are moonbeams anyway? Beams of the moon.

"The weaver's beam . . ." Where is that from?

The Bible? Shakespeare?

I don't know why that comes into my head — I don't have one. Wait a minute, "He beat me grievously, in the shape of a woman; for in the shape of a man, Master Brook,

I fear not Goliath with a weaver's beam; because I know also life is a shuttle...." Falstaff, *The Merry Wives of Windsor*.

How do I know that? Where did it come from? Are you saying that I can access any information at any time? But how do I stop it? I can learn? How? Apparently Dash King discovered that "weaver's beam" was underlined in de Vere's Bible. And this proves that de Vere must have been the real Shakespeare.

What am I supposed to do with all this information?

I'm afraid, Johnny. I love you, but I'm afraid.

Looking back, I wonder if we should have done it; I wonder if we should have gotten into those costumes and dressed up as moonbeams. Or maybe we should have just left the moonbeams alone.

I don't know. It would help if I knew if I were actually *here*. You say one of the things I must do is lose my affection for dying. Why is it that I am so attached to the notion? I suppose it's because at one time the fear of death was proof that we were alive. Now I don't know what I'm saying or thinking. As long as you don't leave me, then I think . . . how can I be all right? I know I'll never be *me* again. What *was* me? I wish you, or I, or someone, could answer that question.

Just tell me it wasn't our fault . . . for impersonating moonbeams. . . .

At ECW Press, we want you to enjoy this book in whatever format you like, whenever you like. Leave your print book at home and take the eBook to go! Purchase the print edition and receive the eBook free. Just send an email to ebook@ecwpress.com and include:

- the book title
- the name of the store where you purchased it
- your receipt number
- your preference of file type: PDF or ePub?

A real person will respond to your email with your eBook attached. And thanks for supporting an independently owned Canadian publisher with your purchase!